Ride

A Second Chance Single Mom Romance

Pierce Motors
Book 3

Chiquita Dennie

304 Publishing Company

Introduction

Grab some wine and get ready for more spicy, sinful, sexy suspense!

Have you signed up for my newsletter?

Join today and find out all the latest new releases, contests, giveaways, sneak peeks, and more!

www.chiquitadennie.com

Author Inspiration

"Never allow anyone to steal your joy. It doesn't matter how many times someone says you can't do something. Invest in yourself—even if it's just writing down what your goals and plans are. Starting small can lead to bigger things."

—Chiquita Dennie

Latest Releases

Series

<u>Struck in Love</u>

The Early Years-A Prequel Short Story

Ruthless:Antonio and Sabrina Book 1

Savage: Antonio and Sabrina Book 2

Beast: Antonio and Sabrina Book 3

Captivated By His Love:Janice and Carlo

Brutal: Antonio and Sabrina Booke 4

Redemption: Antonio and Sabrina Book 5

<u>Heart of Stone</u>

Broken, Book 1 (Emery & Jackson)

A Valentine's Day Short Book 1.5 Emery & Jackson

Rebirth, Book 2 (Jordan and Damon)

Reveal, Book 3 (Angela and Brent)

Bottoms Up Book 3.5 Jessica and Joseph Short

Renew, Book 4 (Jessica and Joseph)

<u>Cocky Billionaire Boys</u>

Cocky Catcher (Cocky Billionaire Boys Book 1)

Bossy Billionaire (Cocky Billionaire Boys Book 2)

<u>The Fuertes Cartel</u>

Stolen (The Fuertes Cartel Book 1)
Saved (The Fuertes Cartel Book 2)
Betrayed (The Fuertes Cartel Book 3)
<u>Carrington Cartel</u>
Torn: The Carrington Cartel Book 1
Claim: The Carrington Cartel Book 2
<u>Something</u>
Something Gained: A Romantic Comedy Book 1
Something Earned: A Romantic Comedy Book 2

<u>Pierce Motors</u>
Refuel: (Pierce Motors Book l)
Pressure: Pierce Motors Book 2)
<u>Summer Break</u>
Summer Nights: (Summer Break Book 1)
<u>TN Seal Security</u>
Aydin: Book 1
Nasir: Book 2
Nicco: Book 3

<u>Standalones</u>
Until Serena(HEA World Novel)
Temptation
She's All I Need
I Deserve His Love
Mutual Agreement
Scoring with Sadie
Exposed (A Bodyguard Novel)
Love Shorts: A Collection of Short Stories
Red Light District(A Fantasy Romance Short)

A Note to Readers

Some characters appeared in *Refuel*, but you don't have to read *Refuel* to understand this book. Each book in the "Pierce Motors" series is a standalone story.

Disclaimer

This work of fiction contains strong language and explicit sexual content and is only intended for mature readers.

This story may contain unconventional situations, language, and sexual encounters that may offend some readers.

If you're looking for sweet, fluffy romance, then I would recommend another book.

This book is for mature readers (18+).

Synopsis

Amena finally had her dream job as a top stylist when her world came crashing down around her. Now a single mother, she was determined to get her life back on track and be the best mom to her sweet little boy. Amena heads home for support from her family and comes face to face with her past.

Laikin worked hard on the racetrack but played even harder off it. Fame, fortune and fast women were all his for the taking. And take, he did. That was true until the day he pulled over to help a beautiful woman and her son stranded on the side of the road. Amena.

He never forgave her but he could never forget her. Now he has to decide how to keep her.

Chapter One

Laikin

Sweat dripped down my forehead; some slipped into the corners of my eyes. Breathing slowly, the adrenalin rushed through me, and my helmet made me feel like I was shut inside a box, hearing the echo of the loud, roaring engine gain volume as my stomach knotted and I passed the first round. Almost immediately, I could hear the screams and cheers of my family in excitement of me winning. I could feel the flashes of cameras picking up on the number 19 painted on my black and red car. When I got the call, my dreams came true, and I stuck with that number because I worked hard and focused from the age of nineteen to make it in this business. I wanted to take the reins, become the best in the business, and show why I was meant to be there. My parents came out to watch, giving me encouragement and motivation to be the best and win.

"Shit." The grip on the wheel felt off after the last pass on the track, and I tried to calculate and strategize how to get around the two rival cars ahead of me, when another car swooped in and made it to the finish line, as reporters, fans, and announcers called another name.

* * *

As I drove down PCH thinking back on my earlier time racing, I turned up the volume on my old school Tupac CD and tapped my finger against the steering wheel, ready for my next race. I met Malik Pierce through my closet friend, Kash, and we became like brothers after signing with Pierce Motors. In just a few years, I have seen my life take off beyond my wildest imagination. The rush from the crowd and the excitement behind the wheel were too much for me to imagine living without them. Only drawback is the press never relenting and always trying to get into my personal business. Every other day, they portrayed me as some playboy partying with women and having sex with them. I cursed, not wanting to be stuck in a traffic jam, as I dodged around the curve, but seeing a woman on the side of the road wasn't something I could leave to my conscience.

I put my car in park, then stuck my head out the window to see if she needed help. "Hey, do you need some help?" It was a pretty nice day out, the wind was suddenly sweet, the pungent air not overly hot or cold with the breeze from the ocean. The female driver was bent over the hood. Even being covered up, I could see she had a nice figure. I snatched the keys out of the ignition, climbed out and eased toward the rear. She rubbed her hands together, glancing at me.

"I do, my car ran hot...Laikin—"

"Amena." I moved slowly, balancing my head and heart to work in sync, and stepped closer, shocked at seeing the past right in front of me. We both stood frozen. My throat was dry, not knowing if this was real or a dream.

"Mommy, I'm hungry," a tiny voice called out.

Amena glanced over her shoulder, flushed but remained silent.

My head whipped around to the back seat, jaws clenched and eyes slightly narrowed. "You have a kid."

She opened and closed her mouth, then whispered, "A son."

I watched her go to the back seat, open the door, and speak with him for a few minutes. I raked a hand down my face. "Where are you heading?" I controlled my anger; today was supposed to be simple, not complicated because of an ex.

"To my friends' place in the city, I just moved down here." Amena walked around to the driver's side and stuck her hand through the window to turn the key in the ignition.

No sound came about, letting me know it wouldn't start. "Looks like you're not getting far. Grab your things and I can give you a ride."

Amena turned on me with a sudden flash of defensive spirit. "I can't ask you to do that, Laikin."

The maddening inability to break free from the past was rearing up again. "Why not?"

"It's not your responsibility."

I hated her high cheekbones, oval face, and soft prettiness that made any man drop to his knees to give her anything she needed.

"Amena, you're in the middle of the highway, with a kid, during afternoon traffic. Either you come with me or stay here and wait for car service."

"You're right."

That same tiny voice yelled again. "Mommy!"

"Okay, Mommy's coming." She breathed out in frustration.

I cleared my throat and folded my arms. "What's his name?"

Amena's face showed a hint of sensitivity when it came to me asking about her son. "Why?"

Those soft lips I remembered nibbling to keep her from pouting whenever she got into a fight with her parents were pressed together. Our past was just that: the past. So the car ride was what I could offer to put my conscience at ease. If she were any other woman, I would do the same thing.

"Amena, we go way too far back to have this much animosity." Yeah, I had a right to be pissed off, but we wouldn't be around each other long enough to dig into old wounds.

She gathered her purse, cell phone, and ushered her son out of the car seat saying, "You mean like breaking my heart?"

"I recall something differently."

A tiny hand pointed at me. "Who are you?"

Amena giggled and I dropped down to his height. "Laikin. What's your name?" I stuck my hand out to shake.

When I asked him a question, he glanced up at his mom before answering. I could see the little hint of her in him from the small round nose, dimples in each cheek, and pointy ears. I used to make fun of her ears growing up and she'd get on me about my failed dance moves. Being my best friend's sister brought her into my life between the ages of fifteen and twenty—until she left with her secret boyfriend, breaking my heart in the process. Brett, her brother, still stayed in touch to this day and we hang out when our schedules are free. As hard as I wanted to ignore those memories of running up behind her at fifteen to give her our first kiss, we needed to get off the side of the road.

"What's your name, baby?" Amena rubbed a hand through his curly hair.

He scratched his nose, and he answered, "I'm Kayne."

I chuckled at his smile. "Nice to meet you, Kayne." Standing to my full height, I motioned to my car and opened the back door to help Kayne climb inside. I watched Amena help him into the back seat. I held the door open to let Amena get in front. When we were fifteen and planning our future together, I thought I would be opening the door for her forever. I locked my seat belt and checked traffic in the side and rearview mirrors. I turned the volume low on the radio and caught Amena scanning my every move before I focused on the road again. I swore the day I saw here again I'd let her know how she fucked with my head when she left town and never said a word to me.

"Mr. Laikin, do you like pizza?" Kayne raised a right hand up in the air, holding tight to his toy in left hand. Even though Amena was fucking up my head right now, her son sat back in his seat with his toy, getting comfortable.

I glanced at him through mirror. "I do."

Kayne kicked his feet up in excitement. "Me too! Mommy, can we have pizza?"

"Kayne, that's not how you ask for something, and besides, I planned on cooking when we got home."

"He's fine."

Amena turned in her seat to look at him. "No, he's spoiled."

"But, Mommy..." Kayne crossed his arms around his chest, poking out his lip.

"Spoiled." I chuckled, thinking back on Amena constantly throwing a tantrum. If Brett and I went anywhere, she had to be there and have the same things.

"What are you saying?" Trying to size me up, Amena fought back a grin at my words.

We pulled off the highway, taking the short route back to Los Angeles. "Where am I taking you?"

"My parents house," she sighed.

"I thought you said your friends'? Either is cool."

"Yeah, at first my goal was to hit up Winter, but this time of day she's working. Thanks."

"For what?"

"Picking us up."

I hit the turn signal. "No need to thank me."

"I asked Brett about you often," Amena spoke

To hear that she talked with her brother about me and stayed updated on my life was shocking because he never gave me a clue about her—especially not that she'd had a baby.

My jaw went slack. "Yeah, can't say the same."

"Not Brett's fault. I made him promise to keep my life away from you."

I scoffed, gripped the wheel tighter, and clenched my teeth. "What?" Brett at the end of the day was my best friend, not sibling, and we told each other everything. I understood she was his sister, but that was a big secret to keep from me.

"Laikin, you're the biggest celebrity in sports. Every girl has a picture of you on their wall, and the last thing I need is to deal with your harem." She raised her fingers, making air quotes.

"What's a harem, Mommy?"

A triumphant smirk stretched across my face at Kayne catching our conversation. Plenty of times I eavesdropped on my mom and her friends gossiping.

I cackled and Amena groaned, shook her head, then slapped me on the arm for laughing.

"Kayne, what did I tell you about listening to grown folks' conversation?"

I peered through the rearview mirror at him, and he shrugged. If Kayne has Amena's personality, I can't imagine what he got from his dad. Early on I knew having kids with her was a dream, but her mind was always wrapped around getting away from her parents. Brett could do anything, but Amena had a curfew, wasn't allowed to date until she was older, could only have limited friends, and had to go to church every Sunday. When I came along, we'd sneak around when I wasn't with Brett and hang out together. Our love of comic books, movies, and Cheetos made the friendship grow into more, and we dated briefly, before something else caught her eye.

"I date, Amena, same as any other single man. Knowing you have a child wouldn't hurt."

Amena grunted sarcastically. "Single. Okay, Laikin."

"We were friends first."

My phone rang. I noticed Malik was calling and picked it up. "What's good. Malik?"

"Are you swinging by the office?"

"I had no plans to. I've got a few errands to run."

"Do those plans include you posting with some influencer or model?" Malik stayed on me about the women I'm often spotted out with by the paparazzi. I made it clear right in the beginning for any woman, especially if I had date the night before a competition, that we'd have to reschedule until racing was done.

After the media circus when his sister and Kash's relationship became public, along with Malik also getting into trouble, he has gotten onto everyone at the office about reining in their extra activities in public, especially the drivers.

"My personal life is simple. I go to a few events and drive. I mean, your wife handles my PR, so if something is off, take that up with Sarai."

Sarai kept him on his toes, and I loved their relationship, just like Kash and Arianna. Settling down looked good on him, but putting me in that box right now wouldn't work. I liked having the freedom to go where I pleased without having to answer to anybody.

"Simple, my ass," Malik cursed.

Fear and sorrow mingled in Amena's glistening eyes, and she looked away.

"I can run by there tomorrow. I have an errand to handle," I explained.

"All right, be prepared for practice, we have a lot riding on the race coming up."

I whipped my car around the corner a few blocks from Amena's parents' home in Calabasas. Listening to her have a conversation with her son filled my chest with pride. I could tell from the little time we'd spent together in the car how good of a mother she was. That was one thing I'd always known she would win at—no matter where she went in life. A role I expected to be a part of and maybe I held a little jealousy at him not being mine.

Pulling myself out of that trance I heard a car horn behind me, and I flicked my turn single to ease down the road.

"Who was that?"

"Malik, the owner of racing team."

"I've seen a few of your races, you're good."

"Thanks."

Kayne mumbled under his breath, "Mommy."

The depths of how much I loved Amena and cherished every moment we had growing up gave me a long-standing bond that would never go away, but at our age now, she'll never be my girl again after breaking my heart. I never settled on any one girl for long, and they all had Amena to thank for that.

After handling the favor of getting her car fixed and getting her to her parents, it would have to end. It would have to be like she was invisible or lived in another state. We could coexist in California, but anything beyond a "hello" could never happen again.

Chapter Two

Amena

Before I knew what was happening, a rush of old memories of Laikin and my brother hanging around our neighborhood with their friends playing ball popped into my head. My brother had no clue about the crush I had on his best friend. It was something I would take to my grave, and now, years later, sitting in a car with him and my son in the back seat sent my nerves to new heights. I came back into town to start over and get away from my ex-husband Virgil, an asshole who felt like he owned me. Everything had to be to his liking-- how I dressed, the food I made, the way we raised our child. Getting swept up in love and being blinded to the red flags at a young age, I should have listened to my parents when they asked if I really wanted a life with him. I rolled my eyes when I saw Virgil's name flashing across my cellphone for the tenth time. I've been avoiding talking with him since the divorce papers were signed, but I knew I would eventually need to let our son speak with his father. However, at the moment, I needed a break and time to think and to get my life in order.

Laikin Trenton, the first boy I ever loved, held that stare that could get anything out of me. "What's up with you, Amena?"

I was grateful he wasn't a crazy stranger on the highway that picked up us, but at the same time having a reunion under these circumstances was weird. I checked over my parents' old block, slipped down in my seat, and looked in the back to check on my pumpkin. He was knocked out in his car seat with drool running down his chin.

"Surprised to see you driving yourself on the road like a normal person." All of his family and friends knew Laikin would make it in sports, from basketball and track to racing. His parents and mine were close because we all lived in the same neighborhood growing up. From what I'd heard, he moved them to a bigger house after he got signed and had endorsements deals.

Laikin stared at me for a moment before licking his lips. "You still do that?"

I slouched back. "Do what?"

He scratched the top of his head. "Change the subject."

"What are you talking about?" I stared back at him in confusion.

"Nothing, Pepper."

That nickname was the last thing I figured he would call me after so many years. It became his signature joke between us because I loved pepper on almost all the food I ate growing up. I loved spicy foods in general, plus with extra pepper, and it stuck so much that even my family wanted to call me Pepper, but I put a stop to it.

I playfully nudged him with my elbow. "I haven't heard that name in years."

"I'm the only one that should call you that." We parked in front of my parents' two-story home that I hadn't seen since I was in my early twenties. I had stopped visiting, only talking on the phone. I felt like they hated me for leaving.

I shook my head, removing my seatbelt. "Still cocky."

"Are you hungry? I can go grab that pizza for the little guy."

"No, I can handle getting dinner prepared."

"Are you sure? What about the little man? It might be faster to grab pizza."

Nibbling on my bottom lip, I realized we hadn't eaten for a few hours after getting on the flight from Atlanta. I'd had a few snacks, but no real food. My stomach rumbled, reminding me that I was starving, and my parents barely cooked now that it was just them.

"We can order something to eat."

"All right, Pepper, hopefully, Kayne didn't pick up your bad habits." He smiled and I shoved him on the shoulder at his silly joke. Opening my door, I went to grab Kayne from the back seat. Laikin surprised me and removed him from the car seat, then picked up his tablet and jacket. Lifting some of our things, I made a reminder to call the tow truck company to bring my car to the shop and got the rest of our bags.

"I can carry him. I know he's heavy."

"He's good in my hands."

"Amena." I froze at the low grumbly voice, taking in my father's five-ten height, square shoulders, gray beard, and short afro he'd had since I was younger.

He approached the end of the porch and I stepped forward, waiting to see whether the raised eyebrows meant I was welcome or not.

"Come give your daddy a hug, little girl."

Running into his arms, I felt like that little girl who always wanted to be protected by her dad and have his attention and love all the time.

A part of me knew I was wrong for taking off without telling my parents too many details. At the time, I thought I knew everything, and living in my parents' house was stifling.

A throat cleared behind me. Forgetting Laikin, I reached to take Kayne out of his arms, and my dad shook hands with Laikin.

"Is this my grandson looking grown now?" Dad took Kayne, rubbing his back. They saw pictures after the birth, and talked with him on FaceTime, but my son wasn't close to my parents. Partially, it was because of my marriage to Virgil. We couldn't visit my side of the family because he was the priority; it was always all about his career and his family.

Kayne started to fuss, which meant he was hungry and ready to play with his toys. Dad whirled around and headed to the front door. I tried to grab my things out of Laikin's hand, but he refused. My dad sat down on the couch, peering at me and holding the TV remote.

"Amena, when did you run into Laikin?"

"Brock, who are you talking to in there?" Mom shouted, coming into the living room.

* * *

"Why can't I go out with my friends? I'm seventeen."

"Because I said so. When you're grown and pay your own bills then you can stay out longer."

"That's not fair! Brett gets to run around with his friends and be gone all night."

"First off, who are yelling at Amena? My house and my rules. Brett has curfew."

"Yeah, midnight," I mumbled.

"He's a boy. He can handle himself."

I threw up my hands. "You treat me differently. Daddy, say something."

It was Friday night, and my parents wanted me home by nine. I would be eighteen in another five months, but according to them, I still needed to be home before it got dark, and I should have been thankful that they cared.

"Listen to your mother, she loves you, baby." Dad rubbed the top of his head, eating his meatloaf and mashed potatoes.

"I hate it here." I shoved my plate forward and jumped up, letting the chair fall to the ground.

"Keep acting like a child, Amena, and see what happens," Mom snapped.

"I get good grades, go to school, and do babysitting on the side for extra money. Why can't I go out with my friends?"

"The discussion is done. Either sit and eat or go to your room. You are grounded."

* * *

Those old arguments flood my mind as I lifted a hand to wave. "Hi."

"Amena," Mom whispered, hand covering her mouth in surprise.

"Yeah, Mom, it's me."

"Are you here for good?" she asked, taking a seat next to my dad on the couch and running a hand across Kayne's back.

At first, Virgil wined and dined me. I was nineteen and he was twenty-seven. Our early courtship was a dream come true and made me feel alive after seeing Laikin fall into anything that opened their legs when we were younger.

I thought it would be a good idea to come back and start over. My life needed a new start, and my son needed stability. The fights, cheating allegations, and being in the public eye because of my husband's job as mayor had put a strain on our lives.

"We're here for now, Momma." Giving her a long explanation of my divorce would have to come later; the only thing on my mind was how exhausted and hungry I was.

"Laikin, how are you, son? Brett told us you have a race coming up soon." Mom reached over to embrace Kayne. He had fully woken up and I watched him look around the room.

"I'm good, ma'am. If you want to come with Brett, there's more than enough room for everybody." Laikin's phone chimed. Out of habit I watched him remove it from his pocket and put it on silent. Biting his bottom lip and grinning meant it was some girl wanting to meet up.

"Thank you, Laikin, We'd love to come," Mom replied.

His six-foot frame and square jawline always gave me goose bumps. Strong wide shoulders that carried me around the pool when we were younger and full lips that sucked on mine gave chills. His dark, charcoal skin had pierced my soul when I first met him. I was fourteen, and he was fifteen, riding bikes with my brother. Back then I had no clue about loving boys, but Laikin was my hero, best friend, and deep down the first man I wanted to have kids with.

"Brett has my number. Let him know and I'll get you settled. I have to leave. It was nice seeing you all again. Amena, take care of yourself." Laikin gave a goodbye wave and whirled around to the door. Kayne suddenly started to pout and throw a tantrum.

"Hey, Kayne, what's wrong with Grandma's baby?" Mom pulled him on her lap, rubbing his back.

"I want to go with Laikin," Kayne cried, extending his arms out for Laikin to pick him up.

My father wiped his tears, turning the TV to some kid channel and patting his leg to get his attention. Scrubbing a hand down my face, I could see my baby getting attached fast. "Baby, Laikin has to work."

Those bright almond shaped eyes stared at me. "I want to work."

We all chuckled at his hopeful eyes. "When you get older, honey, you can work." I kissed his forehead, then removed my coat and shoes.

"Are you two hungry?" Mom placed him on the floor, while Dad sat watching him.

I dug my phone from my purse to check the time. "We are. My car broke down on the highway. I need to get a tow truck."

"Give me your information and I can have my friend bring it to the shop." Dad picked up his phone to make some calls.

"Thanks, Dad." I gave him my insurance and license, then walked with my mother to the kitchen.

"Does Brett know you're here?"

I took a banana from the fruit bowl to hand to Kayne. "I texted him before our flight."

My mom removed plates from the cabinet. Picking up the glasses and pitcher of water from the fridge, I helped gather everything to eat.

"We have a lot to catch up on, Amena. I'm grateful you made it home safely with my grandbaby." The sad yet stern tone let me know we would be having a long conversation soon. I was a problem child—even though it stemmed from being put in a perfect little box and trying to be what she wanted me to be, instead of making my own choices.

I sighed, nodding my head in anticipation of the judgment coming from her voice. Dad went along with her on some things, but he'd get on me if I stepped out of line and got disrespectful.

"I know."

She wiped her hand on the towel. "He's beautiful."

"Kayne's my entire world." I took the utensils out of the drawer.

"I feel the same about you and Brett." Our eyes locked and I understood her fears, love, and devotion to us when we were younger. Raising my son with his father put things into perspective about living in an unsafe environment in a two-parent household or being a single parent and showing your child that love doesn't need to be defined in one way.

My mom smiled. "Laikin's still cute."

"Mom..." A flashback of his long eye lashes, thick lips, and smooth skin captured that same flicker in my soul.

"I'm not dead. He's sexy and I'm guessing you're single."

I grumbled, taking the plate from the microwave. "Here you go."

A few seconds later, Kayne and my father strolled into the kitchen, and we all sat, holding hands as my father said a prayer. I listened to my parents talk to Kayne about what he wanted to do first in Los Angeles. The excitement in Kayne's voice about flying on the airplane, and meeting a new friend named Laikin put a smile on my face. Maybe I made the right choice to come back home.

* * *

After Kayne played with his grandparents after dinner, I gave him a bath and put him to bed in Brett's old room. The both of us had a long day and needed rest before things would get busy. My mom followed me to the room and wanted to know what was going on with Virgil, and I changed the subject. Talking bad about Kayne's dad only annoyed me more and I was exhausted. from the long day. I set my alarm to get up early tomorrow, then laughed at the message from Winter that popped up on my screen.

Winter: Took you long enough to reply.
Me: Sorry, bestie, I got caught up.
Winter: Just remember you have a best friend waiting to catch up.
Me: Calling you now.
Winter: Good.

Right when I went to click on her number, Virgil called. Again, I ignored him and swiped to Winter's name.

"Finally, you decide to call me," Winter sassed.

"Sorry, friend."

"Where is my little baby?"

"Is that the only reason you wanted me to call?"

"Duh," Winter laughed.

"See, this is going to cause me to hang up on you." I opened the side drawer in my bedroom, seeing an old picture book.

"How is my nephew doing?"

"He's good, in bed now."

"Good, I won't keep you long. I'm annoyed you didn't come over. You could have met my date."

"You had a date?"

"Yep, nothing serious."

"Coming from you, that means he will not get a call back." I flipped through the high school photos of me, a few friends, and Brett.

"Girl, the men out here are trash. He wanted me to look into paying on his child support."

I fell over in laughter. "Stop lying, Winter."

"Listen, I might be a lot of things, but a liar is not one of them. I politely escorted him to the door and wished him good luck."

"How many kids he got?"

"Girl! I didn't ask. The moment he said child, I started walking."

I yawned, feeling myself doze in and out of sleep.

"I can hear the sleepiness in your tone. Call me later so I can meet my nephew."

"Sure Thanks again, Winter."

"No problem."

Winter disconnected her line. I placed my phone on the charger and laid flat on the bed, going back in time to my younger years. Even though I was only twenty-eight, and that wasn't old, it still felt weird to see pictures of myself in high school, happy and carefree with Laikin. I only wished he had put more effort into being a one-woman man, instead of a playboy.

Chapter Three

Laikin

On the way to the Pierce Motors Stadium Racetrack, I got a surprise call from Brett, asking why I didn't mention picking up his sister and nephew the other day. "Bro, you of all people, know when it comes to your family, I will always come through."

Brett grunted, barking at something in the background. "Man, Amena is so hardheaded. You can't tell her nothing."

I hadn't had the chance to sit down long enough to catch up with him because of practice.

"True." I heard laughter from Kayne.

"Kayne's over here now watching his favorite shows. Already have a few chicks who want to babysit."

"Don't tell me you're pimping your nephew for dates." I laugh at his idea of getting a woman, especially when people think I'm the playboy out of the two of us.

"Shit, he's handsome like his uncle. Gotta let the ladies know what the future kids will look like."

"Boy, you stupid. Did Amena get her car fixed?" I

stopped in the reserved section for staff, removed my keys, and took my bag out of the back.

"Pops has his friends looking into it right now. Happy she got away from the fuck up husband of hers."

Something about his words caused me to clench my fists, ready to ride out to Atlanta to kick his ass for touching what's mine. "Did he hit her?"

"From what she says, he never hit her, but I put nothing past Virgil."

Displaying my badge, I walked through the doors of Pierce Motors racing stadium, throwing a hand up at a few employees. Being a high-profile athlete came with perks, but everybody treated me like a normal guy. I appreciated it because the world put out too many lies.

Virgil and Amena's relationship surprised everybody. When I was younger, I know I played games, but when we decided to be together, I committed to our relationship. Somehow, she got it in her head that I was dating around—or maybe the friends she had talked her into wanting to break up. After we ended, she sprinted off to be with Virgil, and suddenly she was a wife at twenty.

Putting work in the forefront, I decided to no longer fall in love and focused on my career to get to where I am now as one of the highest paid racing drivers in the world. Both our parents still hung out from time to time, but I stayed away until a birthday celebration came up.

"Virgil's still putting on a show like he's a happily married man, lying through his teeth right now."

I came off the elevator with security in front of me. "What's he saying?" I approached Malik's office door, thanked the security guard, and winked at his secretary. She smirked and pushed the button on her desk to let me enter. I left my bag on the side of the door and slouched down in the chair. Malik stopped typing, glared at me and shook his head.

"Same as usual, He's working for the people to deflect from talking about his family."

"Let me call you later. I made it to the track. I'm about to get some runs in before Malik loses his mind."

"Tell Malik thanks for the tickets."

"For sure." I smiled at Malik, put my cell in my pocket, and leaned back against the chair, having a stare-off.

A grim expression marred his face. "Three different blogs want to run a story about you dating some model who was caught leaving your hotel room with no shoes, her hair all over her head, and in a Pierce Motor shirt."

I held a spark of delight in my eyes because Malik acted like he wasn't out here fucking around before he got married. Hell, a few times, we swapped women. Malik's been a great friend, and I hated to stress him out. Becoming the CEO of a billion-dollar business was a lot of pressure in general, but when you're a Black family-owned business, your expectations to succeed are higher.

"I hear you, Malik." The groupie mentality from women in the racing industry is big, in all sports really, but something made it extra crazy when it came to driver.

"Do you? Only so much Sarai can clean up. We've learned from Kash how it turned out." The tense lines on his face relaxed.

I scratched the side of my head and sighed. "Promise, I will get a better handle on my personal outings."

"Glad to hear we're on the same page. Now, before you go to practice, we want to have you do a commercial."

"Who is it for and how much?"

Malik passed a stack of papers to me. "A jewelry company is interested in you."

"Jewelry?"

"The board thinks it would be a good look to bring in more female viewers. Women love jewelry and since you're single, it gives the illusion to that demographic that you're—"

"Attainable."

"Exactly."

A devilish look crossed my face. "Basically, you want me to lie."

"Never say never."

"Shit. I will leave marriage for you, Kash, and Jackson." I named off his older brother who started the company and signed me to the franchise as I flipped through the documents. I got to the amount of money they're offering and whistled.

I stroked my cheek, ran both hands to the back of my neck and clasped them together. "Five million."

Malik's free hand moved to grab his cup of coffee. "One day's work." He clapped his hands together in amusement.

With a surprise in my voice, I blew my lips together. "A national campaign."

"Come through after practice. We're going to a birthday party." Malik and Kash kept a small circle of friends. Not too many people get the chance to say they're friends with multiple billionaires on paper, but who act like normal people in front of you with the same problems.

I drummed my fingers on top of his desk. "For whom?"

"*Essence*, Sarai's friend."

I flung my hand out. "Sarai is going to start her shit."

"Sarai can speak for herself, and yes, we have shit to discuss, Laikin." Sarai slammed the door behind us.

The slap to the back of my head was our normal routine when I pissed her off with my personal dealings that get me noticed by the media. "Hi, Sarai."

Malik stood and reached for her hand to sit in his lap. "Babe, you're pregnant, no stress." For a married couple, they were more like best friends and he never let Sarai felt like she was alone in raising their child, while they both had high profile careers. Her brown skin glowed under his admiration.

Sarai leaned her back against Malik. "Laikin, why do you make my work harder? We discussed you being more discreet."

"Sis, I promise to behave."

"Stop lying," Sarai snickered and Malik raked his hand over her pregnant belly.

"How far along are you?"

"Six months. Oh, that reminds me. The invite is coming in the mail."

The moment Malik snatched up Sarai, she made a big improvement in his life. Her cousin tried to scam Malik by making false harassment accusations. Sarai worked as his Publicist and got him the best team to find out the truth, which was all about jealousy of Sarai and Malik's relationship. Once they became a solid team Sarai began fixing up not only his life, but his office, making it more layered, with a husky oak table, a carpet to match the drapes, and showcased art pieces on the walls. "Since when do men hang out at showers?"

"Since now! It's a co-ed shower to find out what we're

having," Sarai informed, standing up and walking around the desk in front of me.

A lopsided grin turned into a full-blown victory smile. "Can't I just get you a present and call it a day?"

"Nope." Sarai slipped her phone out of her skirt pocket, typing away.

I rose from the chair and slapped hands with Malik, holding onto the contract with my other hand, and faced them both.

"Sarai, what do you think about the jewelry company, Maze, asking me to do a commercial?" I bent down to pick up my gym bag.

"I told Malik to get the offer, something simple to make you look softer to the public."

Malik held the door open for her to leave. She gently patted me on the arm, and Malik chuckled like a child who was watching his friend get in trouble.

"Women love me no matter what, not my fault."

I walked alongside Sarai, stopped in front of the elevator, and pressed the button, waiting for the doors to open.

Sarai moved with grace and confidence. "Love and sex are two different things, sir." Sarai ignored me, going to her office.

"Sex is all I need!" I shouted and a few gasps spread throughout the floor, making all the women stare at me.

A beautiful woman hiked up her skirt, put her hands on her hips, and offered, "I can help you with that."

I leaned against the wall, twirled my finger around for her turn in front of me. "I bet you can."

"Laikin!" Sarai screamed my name, making me jump as the elevator dinged. I climbed inside, stretched my hand up pretending it was a phone and mouthed *call me.*

*** * ***

Hearing the roar of the cars lined up against the side ready to take off, I checked my gloves and helmet, and walked up to my favorite girl I like to call Princess.

"Talbot, Princess ready?" Stepping into the sun filled afternoon to do a few laps always gave me a peace of mind.

Giving him a fist bump, he stood back, and I climbed into the car, checking all my equipment.

Talbot stalked to the front of the car and lowered the hood. "Princess is ready. Are you coming out tonight?"

"Malik told me about the party, but I need to rest before the big day."

Talbot smirked, which meant he knew that I was bull-shitting him. Meeting him through Kash and Malik made him a brother from another mother. Often, he'd be out with me on some of my adventures at the clubs. The camera only wanted a shot of me, and he liked to be in the background.

"Rest my ass. You have plans to get some ass tonight?"

Although at my big age of thirty, I should be thinking of marriage and kids I was not letting the past drown me. Responsibility came with those attachments though, and right now, I was curious to travel and expand my brand and investments so I could retire by the time I hit fifty with no cares in the world.My phone rang suddenly from my passenger seat and I picked it up and saw Brett's name on the screen. Before I pulled into traffic, I put him on speakerphone.

"He better need something important," I mumbled to myself.

I pulled up to the light and asked, "Hello?"

A small voice came through the phone. "Laikin."

"Who is this?"

"It's Kayne. Where are you?"

Feeling like I was in trouble, I smiled at Kayne checking on my whereabouts. "At work, Kayne. Where's your uncle?"

"He said I can call you."

A question lingered in Talbot's eyes.

"Okay, are you good?"

"I want to see you, and Mommy said you're probably working."

A knot caught in my throat. Amena was put on the backburner of my mind after I dropped her off. The second I walked out of her parents' home, I'd made my mind up to not look back, which would only get those same old feelings started again. Hearing Kayne calling looking for me made me smile.

The worry on Talbot's face turned up a notch as he listened in on the call.

"Buddy, where's your mom?'

"Mommy's working too."

I felt my lip twist in a snarl. "Working where?"

Talbot tapped on his watch to let me know it was time to get started.

"I don't know." Kayne laughed at something and the phone rustled in the background so I pulled it closer to my ear.

There was a sweet edge to her voice. "Hello?"

"Amena."

"Sorry he called you. I told Brett to keep him off the phone," she explained crisply.

I could hear my voice brimming with distaste. "Is that all?"

"What do you mean?"

"Kayne said you informed him I'm too busy to talk with him." It nearly took me a split second to remember we'd talk on the phone often during school. Amena had strict rules growing up. She wasn't able to go out past eight pm, and on the phone, I'd snap a lot thinking it was unfair. With her son wanting to call me, I'd hate to have that same feeling again.

Amena tried to speak in a neutral tone. "Laikin."

"Keep your personal feelings out of it."

"Excuse me?" she snapped.

"Kayne's a kid. If he wants to hang out, I don't mind." No, I never planned on spending all my time with the kid, but he was pretty cool when we met, and I could see that he needed a friend.

"Laikin, we used to be friends. I'd hate to curse you out about my child," Amena continued in a biting tone. I heard background noise from a TV.

"Friends, right. Amena, I have to go." Not waiting for her to respond, I hung up and tossed it to Talbot to put in the bag, then secured my gloves.

Signaling I was ready to go, everybody moved to the side and I pumped the gas waiting for the countdown to begin.

"Show them what you got," I mumbled to myself and took off on the track at a high speed, watching the times on the clock maneuver for another few laps before coming back to the garage. Going to get cleaned up, I left the car with the team to check over and showered before meeting the guys.

* * *

"To the new season, bro! You looked good out there," said one of my pit crew members and best friends, Colson. He was holding a bottle in the air and letting a stripper dance on his lap. After my test runs, we decided to kick back, have a few drinks, and see some ass before my schedule got too busy.

I threw another stack at Remy, the head dancer, and watched her turn around with her ass in front of me. I slapped her ass a few times as she sniggered and crawled back in my lap.

She flipped her long red hair to the side. "Come home with me."

I caressed her cheek. "Remy, we both know you. It ends up with you running." The soft curves of her hips in the black thong held a hidden treasure.

I ignored the roll of her eyes and pressed lips. "That was one time, Laikin."

"One is too many." A flash bulb went off, which caused me to move her to the side, hop up from the couch, and grasp the sneaky photographer that got in our section. I glared at the security guard who was not doing his job and shoved the guy toward him.

"You motherfuckers never leave me alone!" I slammed the camera on the ground and stomped on it as another camera went off, letting me know that his boys had snuck inside.

I smashed the camera on the ground until it broke.

"Ah shit," Colson uttered, knowing I hated photographers. Being in the spotlight came with perks, and I handled it well and did the normal interviews and magazines, but constantly getting in my personal business was off-limits.

"Aye, man, you owe me for that," the photographer

spat, trying to grab the broken pieces. I waved for the main bodyguard, Lee, to get him out of here.

"Take him out and make sure he's squared away."

I passed him a few dollars to pay him off and reached for the bottle to take a sip, then grasped Remy and brushed against her ear.

"You going to put in work tonight?"

She shivered in my arms. I bit my bottom lip, stared down at her curvy 5'6" frame, and ran my tongue against my lips.

"My boy, we're out." I slapped hands with Colson, letting him close out with the other crew, and left the VIP and headed down the stairs to our waiting cars. Tonight, I went out with a driver since I knew someone would be coming home with me. Remy and I stumbled into the backseat to avoid more exposure. My driver held the door open, and I helped her hop in, not wasting time.

"What about my clothes?"

"Fuck those clothes. I got you."

Remy tried to kiss me on the lips, and I moved my head to the side.

"Are you still not going to kiss me on the mouth, Laikin?" Remy's voice sounded like someone had vacuumed a parakeet out of its cage.

"Remy, we've been down that road. I don't do the kissing thing. If you can't handle the situation, you can get out."

I leaned forward and tapped the partition to tell my driver to wait when he started the car to leave.

Remy grasped my arm. "No, baby, I just thought we meant more to each other."

"Since when?"

"Damn, I thought since your dick has been down my throat a few times, you could kiss me on the lips."

"Remy, I don't even kiss your pussy. We fuck and that's it. Anything beyond that will not happen. Are we staying or going?"

Ignoring my warning, Remy got on her knees and unzipped my pants. I tapped the partition and motioned for the driver to leave the strip club.

Chapter Four

Amena

I was cradling Kayne in my arms, and Virgil was once again berating me for not being ready on time. It was sending me into a spiral, and I wanted to hide.

Yanking his suit jacket off the rack, he asked, "Are you even listening?" The snarl on his face sent shock waves through my body. Everything was moving too fast, and all I'd asked for was time to recoup after having the baby.

"Virgil, just go without me." I kissed Kayne on the forehead, soothing him while he was coughing. My baby boy had a terrible cold, and his father thought he needed to man up—whatever that meant.

"How many times have we discussed my career, Amena?"

I sighed, not ready for another lecture on the mighty Virgil Especot's life.

"Since the moment you put a ring on my finger."

"I don't care for your tone." A frown formed right as a knock came at the door and the fake happy husband appeared. "Mr. and Mrs. Especot, the car is ready," Virgil's assistant Sharon explained with her breasts spilling out.

Virgil grinned, not even caring enough to have some type of decorum in front of his wife. We've been married for five years and together eight with our first child and somehow, I became the person I hated. Anything I did, the way I dressed, the way I acted was not the way Virgil wanted his woman to be in the public.

"Sharon, we'll be right down."

"Okay, Virgil," Sharon replied, and my eyes widened in surprise. None of his staff were permitted to call him Virgil and suddenly she had become more comfortable being in our personal business. She stood off to the side with the doorway open and smirk on her face.

"You can go," I dismissed her, rubbing my baby's back.

"Of course, Amena." Sharon sighed, her eyes flinging from me to my husband.

At Virgil's nod, she reached to close the door and I knew he'd start on me about talking to her with a n attitude.

"Let's get something straight, Amena."

I walked to my side of the bed and laid Kayne down, with pillows around him, and planted a kiss on his forehead.

My imagination ran off the charts recalling all of his late nights not coming home and constantly ignoring anything that had to do with me and his son.

"Virgil, I—"

The dark gaze in his eyes and finger pointed in my face let me know it would be another night of fighting. "Shut the fuck up. Somehow you believe you run this marriage and household, but let me be clear, you don't."

"I'm clear on a lot of things, Virgil, and you sleeping with Sharon is not one of them."

Standing with a snide grin, he said, "Yes I am." He

pushed a piece of hair behind my ear, tracing a finger down my cheek to lift my chin.

I forced myself to not throw up my lunch at his admission. Even though we hadn't been in the best place for the last year, I thought we loved each other.

"You lost the right to touch me." I yanked back from his grip.

Virgil shook his head, turned around, stalked toward the door, and stopped with a hand on the doorknob. I admired the tall, broad shoulders that I loved to wrap my arms around and cuddle up against when we first started dating.

"Get yourself together, and the car will come back to pick you up."

The past few years I loved a man who never cared about me, only how we looked in the public. "I told you I'm not going. My son is sick."

"The nurse will watch him. If you skip out, be prepared for the consequences." Virgil yanked open the door, slamming it against the wall, and my son started crying again. I rushed to pick him up and rock him back to sleep.

* * *

"Amena, did you hear me?"

I smiled, tossing the rest of the trash in the garbage and letting go of the memories of my marriage. "No, sorry Budda."

"Where is your head?" He twisted up his nose, leaning against the counter.

"Is my car ready?"

"Changing the subject won't work, lil sis." Brett had

tried many times to harp on me about the men that I dated. The reason I never told him about Virgil and me was to avoid the interrogation we were having right now.

"Budda, my head is fine. I need to start looking for a place to stay and get back to work." He hated it when I called him by his childhood nickname.

"Are you going to tell me why your ex-husband keeps calling my phone?'

I groaned. "We're divorced, so block him."

"Divorced and you kept the wedding day a secret from your family."

"This is why I hesitated to come here." I reached for the soap and sponge to clean up the dishes after I made lunch.

"Amena, stop playing. Did he hit you?"

"Budda."

Brett shut off the faucet, grasped my hands, and turned me around to face him. "Aye, what did I promise you?"

The mental obstacles of my marriage had really put a strain on my communication with my family. Growing up, Brett was my hero, and I had shut him out, along with my parents. "You promised to always be here for me as my big brother."

"Exactly, which means if a motherfucker hurts you then..."

I laid my head on his arm for a brief second. "You hurt them." We both smiled and hugged for a moment, then he released me.

Kayne shouted, "Hi Laikin!"

Brett and I were startled at the surprise pop up of voices coming from the living room. We headed in the direction of my son letting somebody in without waiting for permission.

"Where's your uncle, lil man?" Laikin seemed to get even more handsome as he aged.

I closed my eyes, stomach clenched at hearing *his* voice.

Brett kissed my forehead. "We're going to talk about this later on."

All I could do was nod and follow his lead, letting the conversation hold until were alone. My brother worked as a gaming designer, and I was in fashion. Our parents had reservations about our careers, but once they saw how accomplished we had become, they dropped their concerns. Kayne held one of his toys in front of Laikin's face.

Kayne pointed at Laikin. "Mommy, my friend, Laikin, is here."

"I see that, sweetie pie." I smiled, admiring Laikin's attention on Kayne. Based on his dark tinted shades, black jeans, leather jacket, and jewels around his neck, he must be ready to hit the streets with a woman.

Laikin and Brett did their signature handshake and watched Kayne. I reached down to start cleaning up my things to prepare to leave.

"What's up with you?" Brett wondered, waving at him to take a seat.

"About to head into a commercial shoot." Laikin stretched his legs out wide.

"For whom?" Brett snatched up the remote to change the channel away from *Blue's Clues.*

"A jewelry company." Laikin seemed pensive, not disturbed or angry from our earlier phone call.

"Nice, what are you wearing?"

He shrugged, removing his glasses. "Shit, I have no clue." Laikin released a sigh and ran a hand down his face.

"You know, lil sis is into styling celebrities and shit," Brett announced, and I froze with a hard glare. My goal was to take a few small jobs with some old clients and find a place for me and my baby. Stepping back full force in the spotlight with Laikin would only cause me unwarranted problems.

"Budda," I grumbled, tossed the last toy into the toybox.

"What? You need a job, and my boy has a commercial. It's the best way to make a name for yourself."

Unfortunately, it made sense, but Brett had no idea about the history between Laikin and me.

"This would be perfect, Amena. I can take Kayne to get checked into the daycare, while you go with Laikin to do the gig. Besides, you want to start fresh, right?"

Laikin stared at me with an unamused facial expression.

"They probably already have people to style him." I shrugged, picking up the rest of Kayne's books.

Kayne stood off to the side and looked from me to Laikin.

"Come on, Kayne, time to head out."

"If you want to do the shoot, that's not a problem. Just be prepared to work," Laikin informed me and I felt like it was jab.

"What is that supposed to mean?" Styling has been a passion of mine for many years. He knew my skills, and even when my ex didn't want me going to school, I did it anyway and hustled my way to work with big names.

"Brett, my boy, let's connect in a few days. If you're

coming, then I suggest you meet me there." Laikin dapped up my brother, rose from the couch, high-fived Kayne, and walked out—without giving me any details about the location.

It seemed like no matter what I did, he disregarded my presence. I plopped on the couch and sighed.

"What's going on with you two?" Brett questioned.

"Nothing."

* * *

I laughed with my friends as we walked through the kickback into Skinny P's family home in Balwin Hills. Loud music echoed off the walls. My mom would have a heart attack if she knew I was not at the sleepover with some friends from school. Laikin promised he would stop over, and I found out through another friend at school that he was at a house party with my brother. We would chill together secretly, so I put on my shortest shorts and crop top showing my belly ring. At school I dressed a little more conservative, especially because my brother was known to get in someone's face if they tried to step to me.

"There's your man, Amena." Shelly nudged me in the shoulder and passed me a cup of spiked punch. I glanced in her line of sight, narrowing my eyes at Laikin letting some bitch stand in his face with her hand on his chest. I stomped over, ignoring the whistles and guys trying to stop me.

A fierce heat burned his eyes.

"This is what we're doing, Laikin?"

His face fell into a frown. "What are you doing here, Amena?"

"I'm surprised Mommy and Daddy let you out,"

Snooty Brianna chimed in, giving her two cents, always trying to get in between me and Laikin, and tossed her hand on her hip.

"Fuck you, Brianna. Go brush your teeth and get the cum off your lip." Embarrassment reddened her cheeks.

A few of my girls snickered behind me.

"Amena." Laikin reached for my hand, and I backed up.

"No, you think I'm stupid or something? How many times do I have to catch this bitch in your face?" I snapped.

"Lower your voice. Brett is here." Laikin cupped my chin to face him and pecked my lips.

"She really can't handle you, Laikin. You need a real woman on your arm." Brianna held a satisfied smile.

I tried to lunge at her, but Laikin bear hugged me and walked me out of the party as the crowd started to notice.

* * *

Even though Brett grilled me for answers about Laikin's clear attitude, I chalked it up to Brett being pissed about my ex trying to contact me and setting boundaries of them not fighting him because his political career could do damage to them both.

* * *

I got there early, at least two hours before I was scheduled. I was so happy to see a few people who I had worked with in the past, and they made the day better than I could have imagined. Going back to work as a named stylist in the industry would be hard, and many people wouldn't give me a chance. I knew Laikin only did it because my brother had asked him to. For us to be in the same place together and not let the tension get in the middle of the business spoke volumes.

Dark brown eyes glared at me while I stood near the camera equipment with the director. The hair and makeup team was watching footage of the shoot. Laikin was draped in not only a custom watch and necklace, but diamond earrings hung on both sides. I put him in a dark black suit for the first shoot, and now he wore a leather jacket and blue jeans, shirtless, with him holding a helmet from his team.

"Laikin, you look great. Hold your chin up and look into the camera." The photographer, Grady, moved to the side, pressing record on the camera as the model walked into the shot and moved beside Laikin. Some people might think I had no right to be jealous, and maybe in a rational state that was true, but the dark skin, big boobs, and flat stomach only reminded me that Laikin and I were in different worlds now.

I cleared my throat and walked over to interrupt.

"You said you're free tonight, so dinner like you promised?" she flirted. Laikin scanned my face, and I kept my eyes focused on him as he adjusted his jacket and pants.

"Give me your number after this," Laikin said.

She squealed in excitement and glanced at me. "Girl, tell Laikin I would be the best thing on his arm. We would make beautiful babies." She winked at him, and I put on a fake smile and rolled my eyes.

"You have lipstick on your teeth."

Laikin burst into laughter, and she frowned. She ran

off to the makeup artist. Not wanting to be in his space long, I turned to leave, and he gripped my hand.

"Why you do that, Amena?" He gave me a lopsided gaze.

"What are you talking about?"

Anger contorted the features on his face. "That girl didn't have anything on her teeth. You're hating."

I folded my arms and tapped my foot. "Hating on what?"

"Check it, Amena. Just do your job and we will get along great," Laikin demanded. As the crew started to prepare to continue filming, his co-star stomped back over with a glare on her face. Not wanting to get fired on my first gig back in the business, I moved out of the way and got behind the camera station as the director gave them instructions.

Hours later I held Kayne's hand and the phone to my ear listening to my mother gossip about her friends canceling on her at the last minute. I stepped forward, heading into the first apartment on my list the realtor sent me, and got a shock of my life when I saw Laikin coming off the elevator and not alone.

"Laikin!" Kayne yelled, snatching his hand away and running into his body, not letting him move. The woman sneered at him and stepped back with her hand on her hip.

"Ma, let me call you back."

"Why? Is something wrong with Kayne?"

Not answering, I hung up the phone, approached them to grab Kayne, and Laikin's grin evaporated at the sight of me.

"What's up, Kayne?"

"Who is she, Laikin, and do you have a kid?" the woman demanded, ready to blow up. She's different from the bimbo at the shoot.

"No," Laikin and I answered at the same time.

"Kayne, come on. We have to go." I decided right then and there I would not be looking at the place, even if it was in my price range.

"What are you doing here?" Laikin let Kayne go, and I grasped his hand.

"Nothing, we're leaving."

"But, Mommy, you said we looking at places to stay," Kayne blurted out, telling all my business.

"I thought you were staying with your parents or Brett for a few months." Laikin acted like he was my father and demanded to know everything in my life.

"Laikin, what about dinner?" The woman fussed, reaching for his arm. He moved out of her grip and frowned at her.

"You know we're not like that, Tisha."

"Well, last night you weren't saying that when you stuck your d—" She gulped at his harsh gaze as she almost spilled his private business—which the world already knew—about him being a playboy.

"Kayne, come on, baby." I moved around to leave as Laikin and his little plaything continued to argue.

"Momma, who is Tisha?" Kayne's curious little eyes scanned mine, and I loved how innocently his mind wondered about the world. I hated the man I had a child with, but I would never regret my baby.

"She's Laikin's girlfriend."

"Oh."

Kayne and I left and headed to the next listings of

townhomes and condos. Everything was either crap or too far away from the daycare that I enrolled him in. We headed back to my brother's for the rest of the evening, where we ate dinner, then I gave Kayne a bath and relaxed with a glass of wine.

Chapter Five

Laikin

I could've had Tisha banned from my building, but she gave the best oral sex. For her to get it in her head we would eventually be more was a joke. My life was complicated and busy with my career. Like right now, I stood on a red carpet of the gala fundraiser event taking pictures with two women by my side—my mother and one of many women I called to hang on my arms. My dad wasn't into these things, and I understood; it took me a while to get out to places that didn't entail parties and strippers.

"Laikin, who are you wearing tonight? And we see your momma, but who *else* is your date?" Gossip tea blogger, Alexandria, stayed in my business and she knew posing a question like that would get a cursing out normally, but with my mom here tonight, I would be on my best behavior.

I never liked her because she would always DM me on social media, trying to holla, and whenever I denied her, she'd post a story about me out with another woman, or some cheating scandal, which was weird since I was single. Heat spread through her cheeks at getting a story about me. "My beautiful mom and friend, Callie, are my dates tonight."

"Callie, how are you doing with Mr. Laikin Trenton, billionaire race-car driver? Any plans of marriage and babies?" Alexandria interrogated and Callie giggled at the question because she knew our little sex moments would never become serious.

"Happy to be here tonight with Laikin and his mom," Callie replied, locking eyes with me.

Having had enough of Alexandria's shady interview, I moved my mom and Callie along the red carpet to take pictures for a few minutes, then walked into the ballroom. Mom squeezed my hand to calm me down and I looked at her, smiled, and kissed her cheek.

"I'm good, my queen."

"I know, but never let them see you sweat." Mom picked up a glass of champagne from the server.

"Laikin, where's our table?" Callie peered around the room, remembering Brett was coming tonight as my special guest. I noticed him sitting at a table with a few of my team members and friends. The event was started seven years ago to help support sports, the arts, and underprivileged cities around the country. Sarai, Kash, and Malik created the foundation to give back and I've been one of the sponsors. Social media and the public knew me as some playboy who went from woman to woman, but I gave back and worked on helping the next generation to not fall into a trap of gang violence, jail, or death.

I pointed to our table. "Over there with Brett and Sarai."

"I didn't know Brett would be here tonight." Mom

loved Brett like he was a second child and spoiled him just as much when he used to come for dinner during our youth. Brett always joked about the limelight, and how I was lucky to get to travel around the world with girls falling at my feet. Sometimes it was fun, but it could get lonely, dealing with the pressure.

As we approached the table, I pulled out my mom's chair, then Callie's. I bit my lip to contain my annoyance at seeing Amena with Sarai and her girls. We'd already dealt with each other on set and her showing up at my condo. Now, we were at a big gala together, and Callie was clinging to me, trying to make our closeness out to be more than it was, which would only cause more confusion.

I slapped hands with Brett, then Kash joked about my commercial clips that had been posted online. A few candid moments from behind the scenes got posted and I still had to hear my mother's mouth about me showing off and getting too bigheaded.

My mom hugged Brett. Callie talked with the server, while I stood, briefly talking with my boys to avoid staring at Amena's fine ass in her gold off-the-shoulder dress.

"Bro looking sharp tonight," Brett joked, holding up his hand and pretending it was a camera, taking a photo.

I waved him off. "Man, shut up. Where's my little homie, Kayne?"

"He's with my parents. Amena tried to stay home, but I begged her to be my date tonight. Thanks again for the invite," Brett mentioned, sticking out his hand for a shake.

"Never have to thank me, man. Kayne's cool. I have to get him to the track one day."

Mom held both hands to her chest. "Brett, I know that

is not your sister, Amena. Child, when did you come back to town!"

Brett and Amena chuckled. Mom got out of the seat to give her hug. "Amena, so good to see you. Your mom didn't tell me you were back in town," my mom said, holding Amena's hands.

"It was a surprise to everyone," Amena laughed, shaking her head.

"Kash switch seats with me so Amena and I can catch up. You don't mind, do you, Laikin?" Mom asked, glancing from me to Kash with excitement. I hated how she acted at these events sometimes.

"Ma."

All I could do was smile and take a seat next to her and Amena as Kash changed seats.

"So, tell me: What have you been up to? Is your husband here?" My mom meant well, but sometimes she had a tendency to get off-track and want to know everything in one sitting.

Amena's long lashes fluttered, trying to play off the awkwardness with a faint smile.

"Ma, slow down. The girl just got back in town."

Mom scoffed and waved me off. Most of the crowd started to take a seat and introductions were starting. The money was made off donated items. I gave a few signed shirts and helmets. Kash donated tickets for a race. Amena listened and showed off pictures of her son from her phone, while talking to my mom.

"I saw the final cut of the commercial and you looked good." Sarai approached from around the table. Malik stood off talking to a few bigshots from other teams. Anytime Sarai gave me a complement I embraced because she stayed on me when I fucked up.

"Is this Sarai being nice for once?" I teased, and she pretended to punch me in the shoulder. She extended her arms out for a hug, and Callie gripped my wrist, blocking me. Sarai's head fell back in laughter, and I knew that at any moment, she'd be going off on Callie and hurting her feelings. Never in my life had I looked at Sarai in any way other than like a sister. Callie knew we were not together, only friends, and to trying to lay claim to me in public would only make me drop her and never call again.

"Sweetie, calm down. He's a client only," Sarai informed her, turning to head back to her seat.

"Callie, get a grip. We've discussed this already."

Soon as she opened her mouth, the band started to play, drowning out most of the conversations. Our food arrived at our table. I listened to Mom and Amena, going back and forth in conversation like long-lost friends. My petty side could have hogged Mom's time, but after seeing the smile on her face at the pictures of Kayne, I avoided being an asshole.

"Honey, have you seen Kayne? She has a little boy." Mom gleamed in excitement.

"I have." I drank the rest of the champagne, then held the empty glass up for the server to replace.

"Amena's going to bring him by for a visit soon."

I nodded and continued to ignore the hate coming from Callie on my right side. Amena sitting next to Mom only put more tension in the air, especially with Mom fawning over her. The spotlight flicked around the room watching a few kids smile at seeing some of the sports heroes in person.

"Ladies and gentlemen, next up for bidding is the opportunity to visit the racing track with Laikin Trenton, one of the biggest drivers in the industry and two-time champion," Gizelle explained. She was the main announcer and an editor from the world of fashion, sports, and art.

I stood up and waved as the bidding started at Ten thousand dollars. A few photographers took shots. Some of the guys from the team approached, and we shook hands.

"Yo! Laikin, bro, hook me up with your friend," Sincere, one of the other drivers, suggested.

I looked at who he was staring at—Amena, giggling with her brother—and I shook away the thought. "Off-limits."

Sincere grinned, rubbing his hands together. "Off-limits because you have that on lock or off-limits because she's married?"

"Sincere, dude is gonna kick your ass if you try his women," Clarence jested, patting me on my chest.

Sincere waved off the comment.

My warning tone was confident and unmistakable. No, I didn't want her—the last woman on the planet for me would be Amena—but that didn't mean I wanted to see her date my friends, either. "Off-limits means off-limits, my boy."

"What's up, Callie?" Sincere flirted, licking his lips at her, and I should of have been pissed, but Callie meant nothing to me. I had no fucks to give. As long as he kept Amena off his radar.

What am I saying?

She's a grown woman.

"The bidding for an hour-long visit on the race track with Lakin Trenton is now closed in the amount of seventy thousand dollars."

The entire room erupted in applause. I marched over to the stage and hugged the older brown skinned woman and shook hands with her husband. My donation would help, and seeing us hit close to Four hundred thousand this year was amazing. Every time I visited different youth centers, the look in their eyes as they thought about what the future held seemed so far away, and I wanted to make a difference and teach them that nothing was impossible with hard work.

"Baby, can we go now?" Callie met me halfway before I made it to the table and cuffed my arm. The nagging got irritating.

"I need to grab my mom and check with my people before we go."

"How long is that going to take?" Callie pouted, fixing my tie.

Removing her hands from my chest, I sighed in frustration. All night she'd had snarky comments and a pissed off attitude.

I swallowed hard before asking, "What's up with the attitude?"

"I thought tonight we would come out as a real couple."

"Since when are we a couple?" My neck jerked back in surprise at her suggestion.

"Laikin, it's been three years of fucking and showing up at your events," Callie hissed, getting loud and in my face, causing a few people to stare at us. Tamping down my anger, I ignored her and walked back to the table to finish hanging with my friends. Callie staggered back to the table, avoiding a few people holding up their phones to get any type of gossip. She sat and waited for me to leave.

* * *

Morning sunlight beamed into my bedroom, and I felt a heavy arm across my back. I slowly popped open my eyes and cringed at seeing Callie cuddled up in my sheets.

"Shit."

Normally I wouldn't bring anyone back to my condo or my house in Malibu, but feeling a banging headache let me know I got too wasted last night. Brett suggested we all go out to the club after the fundraiser and like always I went to kick off some steam. Stretching and sitting up in bed, I gently nudged Callie to wake up.

My stomach revolted in terror at the thought that we didn't use protection. "Callie." I scanned the wastebasket near the bed and saw an open condom wrapper.

"Mmmm, Laikin...fuck me harder," she mumbled, rubbing my chest.

"Callie, time to wake up." I threw the covers back, stood from the bed in only my boxers, and headed to the bathroom to freshen up.

Callie sat up, a teasing smirk on her face. "Laikin, why can't I stay?"

I stepped out of the bathroom with my toothbrush, shaking my head at her sitting up with her breasts out trying to entice me.

After rinsing my mouth and turning on the shower, I came back to grab her things and shoved them in her hand, so she could get dressed. "You already know we're not like that, Callie."

"Your parents and friends like me, on top of what it can do for your brand. Laikin, we can be good together." Callie pleaded, sliding her dress on and slipping into her heels.

"Not happening and take this as our last outing or whatever you want to call it." I kissed her cheek, went back into the bathroom, and locked the door.

Bang!

"I hate you, Laikin!" Callie screamed.

Chuckling, I jumped in the shower and prepared for all the bullshit Sarai would bring my way after last night. If Callie slept over, that meant paparazzi saw us come into my building together, and social media would blow it out of proportion.

Soon as I was ready to leave for the day, I locked the door behind me and almost tripped when I ran into something and dropped my keys.

"Kayne, I told you to be careful with the ball." Amena's sweet voice carried through the quiet hall.

"Laikin!" Kayne stood up, dropped the ball, and wrapped his hands around my legs.

"Sorry about him." Amena tried to grab him, and I tugged her back.

"He's cool. High five, Kayne."

"Are you our neighbor?" Kayne wondered.

His question caught me off guard. "Possibly."

"Kayne, that's rude," Amena chastised.

I glared at her for upsetting him. The anger directed at her shown on my face for dumping me all those years ago, but she kept trying to play the victim, and harping on Kayne for talking to me is getting on my nerves.

"Amena, chill. It's just a question."

"He's a child. I'd rather he stayed out of adults' personal business." She grabbed him by the arm and pulled him off my legs.

Curiosity got the best of me. "Are you moving in here?"

"At first, I thought it would be a bad idea, but the price isn't bad. I have help from my parents, my brother and my savings, plus it's close to Kayne's school."

Kayne dribbled the ball, making me smile. I rubbed the top of his little curls. "That's cool."

As she spoke, I could hear a nervousness in her voice, as if she thought I hated her. "Will that be a problem for you?"

"What do you mean?"

"I saw the same girl you brought to the dinner leave a few minutes ago."

"Why would that be a problem? I'm not married to anyone." I crossed my arms over my chest.

She scoffed. "I mean if you're running women in and out of here, I think I should know."

I chuckled, catching the snarl in her eyes. "Amena, you're something else."

"Something else?" Confusion creased her brow.

"Yeah. Look, I have a meeting in fifteen minutes with my PR team. They liked the looks you set up for my commercial and wanted me to reach out to see if you wanted to do more campaigns," I said, ready to get out of the hallway. Going back and forth about my dating life that she had no right to comment on left a bad taste in my mouth. Her deep brown eyes sent me a signal that I would get hurt again.

"Uhm, I don't have a website or full portfolio. I'm still getting things together and making sure Kayne has every-thing he needs."

"Sarai will hit you up about the details. I have a few interviews coming up and club appearances."

"Fine, just have them send me an email."

"Cool." I squatted down to Kayne's height and

stretched my hand out for a slap. "When I get time, we're going to play a one-on-one match." I playfully picked up his basketball, bouncing it on the ground.

"Yay! See, Mommy? Laikin's my friend."

"Come on, baby." Amena escorted him toward the condo for rent.

I saw the elevator open, and the realtor stepped off coming in my direction.

"Mr. Trenton, good to see you again," Miss Claymont said.

"Miss Claymont, are you showing Amena the last condo rental?"

What Amena didn't know was that I owned the four condos on this floor and rented them out as investments.

"I am. Hopefully, she signs."

"Give her whatever she wants on price."

Her face dropped in shock. "Huh?"

"Amena's my best friend's sister, and she's moving back to town. Give her a break on the price and don't tell her who owns the place."

"Are you sure? They run high in this market."

I knew she was worried about her commission. "Positive and don't worry. You still get your commission."

She nodded and smiled. "If you're interested, then I have a few more buildings that opened up."

"Send them to my accountant as usual. Thanks."

"No problem! Thank you."

I sprinted to the elevator and out of the building, hopped into my Maserati, and moved in and out of traffic, pressing the radio to one of my favorite stations when I came to a red light.

"Laikin, over here! Laikin, is it true you're engaged to Callie Evans?" A reporter hanging out the window of a car next to me pushed a camera in my face for a picture.

Ignoring his question, I pressed the button for the window to roll up, and I rode off as the light turned green.

I arrived at Pierce Motors' offices moments later, gripping my phone as it rang with a call from Brett.

Sincere came onto the elevator with me. "What's up, man?"

Sincere approached and I nodded, listening to Brett speak on the other end of the line.

"I got a call from Amena. She got a place in your building. Thanks for hooking it up," Brett said.

A knot of tension formed in my stomach at the thought of him ever finding out that I'd lied about our relationship. "Of course. She's your sister."

"Getting her a gig as your stylist..."

I smirked, stepping out of the elevator, and stalked down the hall to Sarai's office. "Sarai liked the fit."

He grunted. "If something's going on with you two, I want to know," Brett expressed.

"Yeah, that's never happening... but I have a meeting."

"All right, bro." Brett let go of the tension.

"Yep." I hung up and glanced at Sincere talking with Sarai's secretary. He knew sleeping with Sarai's team would land him in hot water. I gripped his shoulder, pointed to her open office, and he followed with a smirk on his face.

"Not the time, playboy."

"Sincere, call me when you're done," she said, handing him a piece of paper. I snatched it out of his hand and dropped into the trash.

"Do you want Sarai to kick your ass?" My brows

pinched together as I shut the door behind us, taking a seat in front of her desk.

"Sarai, tell your boy you have no problems with your girl out there talking to me," Sincere egged on, picking a piece of candy out the dish.

Sarai cleared her throat, leaning back in her chair with both arms crossed. "Let me think... um... Sincere Pendleton is the biggest industry hoe that I have to field calls from, and bloggers are trying to get interviews about the alleged three DNA tests you had to take only this year. I really don't think he would be a good fit for my secretary."

"Damn!" Sincere shrunk in his seat, covering his face as I laughed.

"Leave her alone, Sincere," Sarai demanded, leaning forward and picking up papers off her desk to pass to me and him.

"Man, you hating, Sarai," Sincere grumbled, snatching it out of my hand.

"No, your momma a hater. Now, focus more on business and less on getting your little pecker wet," Sarai blasted him.

At that moment, I couldn't hold back anymore and cackled at her remark, holding my stomach.

"Fuck you, Laikin," Sincere growled.

"Bro, leave that girl alone."

"Anyway, I have a few things in the pipeline, and I wanted to see you both because one of them has you both lined up for an interview together," Sarai expressed.

"The Maya West talk show? Isn't she married to the Governor?" I remembered reading in the newspapers about a local talk-show host and the governor dating.

They were also friends with Gage Young, who I'd met at a sports award show.

"Correct—even though she's more lowkey because of her husband's position, she's only doing shows on a limited basis. I thought it would be nice to get you both on together." Sarai typed away on her computer.

"We would need to fly out to New York."

"Yep. The sooner the better. It would be a little mini tour. Basically, you're both the stars of Pierce Motors, along with Ledger who I just signed to represent." Sarai stood and walked to her fridge in the corner of the office, then grabbed two bottles of water and handed them to us.

"Ledger's cool people," Sincere said.

"I agree."

"Perfect. I know you have a race this week, and then you're off, so I planned the interview in a few weeks, and I have your plane tickets and hotel set up already," Sarai informed me.

"Sarai, you have me doing back-to-back interviews with bloggers, and you know that's not my style."

"Look, you are still seen as a playboy right now. To combat the drama, I extended a ten-minute interview window—and let's not forget, there are pictures of you and Callie leaving the party drunk." She shoved the magazine in my face from Turnt Up Vibe. Soon as the flash went off that night, I knew Callie and I would be plastered every-where. She had to get shit started by kissing my neck. I groped her ass, and it turned into a make out session in front of the venue while we waited for the limo to pick us up.

"That wasn't my fault."

Sincere slapped me on the shoulder. "Finally, it's not me in trouble."

"Shut up, Sincere. You two will act right and no partying. I have enough work to scrub any mentions of sex tapes being blasted online." She scoffed, turning the computer around for us to see a blurred-out photo with my name in bold letters on Gossip Tea's blog page.

I tried to forecast the probable moves Sarai would need to make if I had something illicit online. "Gossip Tea is lying. I don't have a sex tape."

Sighing, she clasped her hands together and stared at me. "Doesn't matter. As long as your name is mentioned, it's getting interest. So, while I try and get it removed, I need you to play nice."

"All right." A quiet voice told me to keep my real feelings under wraps and not cause any more problems before my next race.

"Let me know if Amena is free. I have a contract for her."

I gave Sarai the contact information. "I will check if Amena's free."

"Will it be a problem for you two to work together? I refuse to have any more issues, Laikin." Sarai loathed the attention that came with dating someone in the business, being the wife of a billionaire and the team's President. Getting noticed beyond the person you're attached to brought problems, and she had nothing to worry about with me and Amena.

"Amena and I are professionals."

"Bullshit," Sincere coughed into his hand.

Sarai and I looked at him.

"With a past," Sarai said with understanding and sensitivity.

Why did she continue the deep dive if she knew what

happened between us. "Then find someone else, Sarai. You know clothing is not my thing."

"No, I want Amena. What she did for the commercial really put you in a better light. Just keep it all business," Sarai replied as the door opened. I whipped my head around to see Malik.

Sincere and I rose from our chairs to leave. "Gotcha."

Malik shook our hands and pulled his wife into a hug. "Everything good in here?" Malik wondered.

"Always, honey." Sarai kissed him on the cheek.

"Great. Sarai told you about the tour?" Malik inquired.

"Yeah, and I hate it, but what can I do?" My cynical inner voice kept telling me to cancel and focus on the goal of winning to get closer to the championship race.

Malik laughed. "She's tough, but worth the headache." Malik ducked when Sarai tried to slap the back of his head.

"Get out of my office, all three of you," Sarai fussed, and I leaned forward and pressed a kiss on her cheek.

Sincere threw up the peace sign. "We're out, fam."

After leaving Sarai's office I headed to the track to get in some practice time before I headed back to my condo to rest and get some sleep. I promised Kayne that we'd hang out, and I wanted to be in a better mindset—especially if Amena got a hold of the news about us working closely together.

Chapter Six

Amena

My money was running low, but I put in a few calls to some of my old friends in the fashion industry to see if anyone was interested in bringing me on as full-time stylist. I loved working with people who let me do what I wanted without question based on their personality. After I did another walk through the condo and talked with my brother and parents, I decided to go with the place—even though Laikin was only a few doors down. Brett was fine since he thought it would provide me with some security in case anyone messed with us. Personally, I doubted that we could even coexist,let alone work together. On the outside, he was acting like he was fine with his PR team asking me to style him again, but his flat answers gave me pause before I signed my name on the lease. Also, the cost seemed really low, and I wondered why the owner didn't put up a fight when they found out I was a single mom starting over. The building came with a lot of amenities like a gym, juice bar, and business area. Ultimately, I wanted to have a house for me and Kayne, so staying for a few years to build up my name again meant more than jumping into purchasing a home right now. Standing in the middle of the room, I smiled with glee, taking in the two bedroom, two and a half bath one story unit.

Grabbing my purse and keys, my hand wrapped around my ringing cell showing Winter's name. Clicking the answer button, I was ready for the harsh words. "I should smack you."

I snorted at her statement. "Why, friend?"

During the last few years of school, Winter came into my life and helped to keep me sane. Winter was my closet friend, next to Laikin and my brother. She was a feisty, spunky, smart, 5'4" tall redhead with warm, honey brown skin.

"Friend my ass, Where is my baby Kayne?" Winter argued.

"At daycare."

"Are you all moved in yet?" Winter had never liked Virgil. Many times, she'd questioned whether I was ready for what he wanted. I used to think that she was like my parents, who hated all my relationships. Truthfully, they were right.

I was hard. Winter was strong. "I am."

"Is he still calling?"

"Of course—from unknown numbers—and making statements like we're a happy family."

"Girl, that man is crazy. How is he getting away with that?"

"A few times his team has put up video or pictures showing us out of town and saying I'm taking care of family, and our marriage is good." Virgil's family had a vested interest in looking good for the public.

"All lies."

I stood in pleased surprise at everything coming together. "It sure as fuck is all lies from his camp."

"Glad you got away and free to get your man back."

I locked up and went to the elevator. It opened, and the maintenance manager got off. We both smiled in acknowledgement.

I pressed the button for the main lobby. "What man, Winter?"

"Amena, stop being dense. Laikin is your man."

"He's not."

"Well, according to me, he will be if you stop acting stupid."

Laikin looked pissed that me and his mom were getting along so well and then to see me again at the condo? I figured he would tell Brett to find me another place. "Laikin and I are friends."

"Friends that want to be more."

"He did get me the job on his commercial. Plus, his team wants me to do another styling job."

"See, already making sure you get paid. Look at God!" Winter barked in laughter.

I came out of the building as soon as the elevator doors opened. I strolled to my car, jumped inside, pressed my phone into its holder, and put it on speaker.

As dramatically as she acted, Winter was right about him making sure I got back on my feet and I would thank him with dinner soon as an appreciation.

"Where are you headed right now?"

"I have to get to the store, grab food for my place, then order some furniture and pick up Kayne."

"Then I will come by once you make it back home and we can catch up."

"Okay, let me text you my address."

"Please don't go missing. Again, friend, happy you're back."

Passing through the streets in my parents' second car, I made a note to thank my dad for letting me use it.

"I won't, friend."

Hanging up with Winter, I accidentally tapped on an incoming call. "Hello."

"Amena, you've had your fun, time to come home," Virgil growled. A loud slamming noise came though the phone.

"Virgil, we are divorced."

"I told you to death do us part and I hold those promises."

"Kayne and I are no longer your priority. Please go be with the woman and child you've kept hidden. She probably would love the limelight."

"Bitch!"

"Goodbye, Virgil."

Before he could say another word, I ended the call, tossed it in my purse, and pulled up at Kayne's daycare.

I stepped out and placed my visitor badge on purse shoulder, then ambled inside and headed for his room. I knocked on the door and the teacher opened it to step outside.

"Hi, Amena. What are you doing here?"

I frowned at her statement. "I came to get Kayne. Is he sleeping?"

"His father picked him up."

"No, how can that be?" I reached around her, yanked open the door, and ran in, scanning the room to find Kayne.

"He came about ten minutes ago and said you were working."

"He doesn't have permission to take my son!" I yelled.

Some of the kids stopped playing and started to cry.

"Amena, please step outside."

"I can't breathe." What I knew at that moment Virgil was getting more and more possessive and if he hurt Kayne to get to me, I would never forgive myself. I took out my phone and dialed his number. It went straight to voicemail, and I dialed again.

Kayne picked up. "Hi, Mommy."

I smiled at hearing his voice. "Hi baby, where are you?" I tried to get Kayne to give me any clue.

There was rustling on the line, and then the gravelly voice of my ex. "He's with his father, the same place you should be."

"Virgil, we both know you barely had any interest in my son when he was born." I ran out of the building and jumped in my car.

"My son is going to be raised in a two-parent home."

I wiped the corners of my eyes with the back of my hand. "How when we're divorced?"

"We'll get remarried."

"Where are you?" The best way to get him to agree was to stay calm.

Virgil loved to torment me. "Meet me at your parents' house."

I jerked back, in shock that he'd go to my parents' home with my child. "What games are you playing?"

"Come and find out." The dial tone came through and I blew my horn racing through traffic.

* * *

As soon as I crossed the highway, I made it to my parents' home in less than twenty minutes. I left the car running and hopped out to see a limo parked out front, along with my mother's car in the driveaway. His security detail stood outside ignoring me.

"Kayne!" I shouted as I ran through the front door and paused at my mother and father sitting with Virgil.

"There she is," Virgil said.

My mind blocked out everything other than getting Kayne back. "Where's Kayne?"

"He's fine. Take a seat."

I walked off and headed upstairs to search for Kayne. "Virgil, we're not doing this here." The thought of my parents helping Virgil crossed my mind.

"He's not leaving with you, Amena." Virgil jumped up from the loveseat and followed me.

"Amena, we're on your side, honey. Virgil says you blindsided him with the divorce," my dad said as he stood from the couch.

"He's lying and trying to manipulate you. Virgil knows that his controlling attitude and possessiveness was too much, and I wanted out. On top of him using us as props."

Honestly, deep down, I knew it had been my choice to stay with him after the first few years of our marriage— even after I saw the red flags of him working nonstop and missing meals, wanting me to put on a fake smile for people on the campaign trail, shaking hands with strangers and making it seem like he was the best man in the world, the one who would bring Atlanta into the future.

Every moment of our life together played in my head from what I ate to only being with his friends and family.

He raked a hand down his beard, his brows pinched together, clearly hating that I was putting our business in the public eye. Virgil growled and stalked forward. I moved back. "The only thing I have done is try to give you a better life. *You're* the one who wanted something different. You were tired of your parents running your life."

"Virgil, watch how you talk to my daughter in my house," Dad barked, stepping in front of me and blocking Virgil.

"Ma, Pops! Where are you at?" Brett coming over right at this moment was not going to end well.

"Let's go, Amena," Virgil commanded, then turned to walk back down the stairs and I followed, hearing Kayne laughing. I stopped at the sight of Laikin, Brett and Kayne, playing around. A flash of anger streaked across the face of Virgil as his fists clenched. The years of terror were still locked deep inside me. Virgil made it seem like his love had brought me into a bigger world, but I couldn't have a life outside of it, and he never supported my dreams.

"Kayne, say goodbye to your mother," Virgil said and extended a hand for him to take. Kayne looked from his father to Laikin.

I closed my eyes, stomach clenched at the pause in his reaction.

Kayne had no clue of what was happening. If looks could kill, the antique pieces on my parents' wall would be shattered by Virgil's head if my brother had a say. "Laikin is my friend; we're playing video games."

Virgil went to grab Kayne and Laikin blocked him.

"That's not how it's going down." Laikin stood in front of Kayne, blocking him from his father.

"Aren't you Laikin Trenton, the guy who races cars for a living?"

"Virgil, please go, and I will call you," I insisted, moving around the living room to pick up Kayne.

The atmosphere was so thick, and I knew that at any moment, Virgil could call his men inside and make it a bigger problem. My parents hated drama, and right now, I was bringing nothing but conflict into their home.

My pulse quickened, I snatched up the keys, pulled Kayne by my side, and started for the door. "Amena, where are you going?" Mom came up beside me.

"Virgil, you and my sister are divorced the last time I heard." Brett's intense stare gave us all pause. I tore my eyes away from Mom to see Virgil and Brett with balled fists at their sides.

"Brett, leave it alone. He's only going to use it as a way to take Kayne from me. Mom, we'll talk later."

"What happens between my wife and me has nothing to do with you." Virgil remained uncomfortably still, then bumped shoulders with Laikin and walked towards the front door to leave. He stopped and glared at me. "Kayne, I will be back for you." Virgil held the doorknob and gestured for his security to follow him to the car. The entire time, my parents' eyes were on me.

"Before you two start, let me take Kayne home and get him fed and into bed. Virgil took him from daycare without telling me, so right now I can't take a lecture." I spilled my entire guts, not letting them answer, then walked out to my car and got Kayne situated in his car seat.

I buckled him in and shut the door. I leaned up and released a breath, then bumped into a hard chest and almost fell before warm hands came around my waist.

"Give me your keys."

"Laikin, no," I said, then backed up to put space between us.

"Amena, I'm driving. You are upset, and Kayne needs you to be clear minded." Laikin held a hand out for my keys, and I sighed.

"Okay." Slouched in the car, I covered my face with my hands in thought, listening to Kayne talk to him from the backseat. A few minutes went by, and Laikin reversed out of the driveaway.

* * *

What I didn't think would happen was Laikin making us come to his place. Once we got home, I took a nap so I'd be in a better headspace. His place was clean and modern, with opulent Chinese art on the walls. A mixture of warm leathers and bright prints.

Laughter echoed throughout Laikin's living room. I watched him sit with Kayne on his game console, teaching him how to play and distracting him from what had gone down. Rather than cooking, he ordered burgers, fries, and chicken strips and that let me have some free time to order furniture for our place and avoid the three voice-mails from Virgil.

The money I had was enough to get everything for my baby's room and the living room basics. With the money from my commercial shoot with Laikin, I bought more clothes and toys for his room.

Shutting down the computer, I stood and headed to the kitchen to set up the food on the table, then poured water for Kayne and grabbed a beer for myself.

"Kayne, time to eat." The clock hanging on the wall

read eight-thirty. Normally I would have him showered and in bed by now.

"Yes. ma'am." Kayne stopped playing the game and came over to the table with Laikin trailing and pulled a chair out to sit down.

"Thanks again for driving us back."

"Mommy, is Daddy coming back for me?" Kayne ate his chicken strips, soft eyes looking at me in wonderment. Protecting him from any harm, including his father, was my job and I refused to let Kayne become like Virgil.

I leaned over to cut up his food. "No, baby. Your dad is not."

"Laikin can be my dad." Kayne grinned.

The last thing I wanted was Laikin feeling obligated to take on the responsibility of being Kayne's father. "Finish your dinner, then bedtime," I rushed out, grabbing the glass of beer and taking a sip. Kayne continued his conversation with Laikin about the next time they would play the game. I listened and smiled at the joy he'd felt in the short time they'd spent together. In another world Laikin and I could have been a family if I had never left to marry Virgil.

* * *

I heard a knock at my window, dropped the clothes in my hand, and jogged over to let him in while I had the guts to see his face. As usual Laikin pulled me into his arms and tried to kiss me on the lips. We hadn't talked since I caught him at the party. He tried calling and talking to me at school, but I avoided him. My friends told me I was too serious about dating him when I should be single. Besides, so many girls had tried to break us up by making it seem like he'd slept with them behind my back.

"Amena, you're still on that party shit?" Laikin sat down in the chair at my desk and stretched his hand out to pull me into his lap.

"Laikin, we need to talk." I rubbed my arms, not ready to tell him the truth.

"Where are you going?" Laikin jumped up from the chair and tossed my shirts to the side of the bed.

"I met someone."

"What?" He hiked up his pants that kept falling down from not wearing a belt.

I avoided eye contact. "I'm sorry, but we can't do this anymore."

"What are you saying?" Laikin closed the space between us, picked up my hand.

"I met...I think it's best we see other people. My parents never wanted me to date until I was older and keeping this a secret from them and my brother is too much."

He shook his head. "Amena, please don't do this to us."

"The party gave me clarity. I think we're both young and being too serious."

His nose wrinkled in confusion. "All this time, you've been seeing someone else? Is that what you're saying?"

"You need to leave."

"Amena, talk to me baby."

I grabbed my suitcase and phone. I felt the vibration of Virgil's text thread. He was outside, waiting. My parents weren't home for the weekend, and Brett was staying at his girlfriend's house. I marched downstairs and paused at the front door, turned the knob, released a long-held breath.

Laikin grasped my hand tight. I glanced over my

shoulder, back to opened front door to see Virgil's blacked-out Mercedes. He was in the process of following in his father's political footsteps. He was older than me at twenty-eight, and I admired how he was going after what he wanted.

"Laikin, I promise to call when I get settled." I strolled out of the house, as Laikin trailed behind me outside.

"Who the fuck is that in the car?" Laikin released my hand and marched down the steps. I ran to jump in front of him.

"Amena, we have to go." Virgil stepped out of his car, smirking at Laikin.

"Who are you?" Laikin balled up his fists.

"Nobody. We need to go, Virgil." I tossed my bags into the backseat and climbed into the car.

He started the engine. "She's my fiancée." Virgil pulled away from my house, and I looked back through the mirror, seeing Laikin's heart sink, triggering a bitter knot of pain in my chest.

Ever since that day I'd left the memories of us in the past and avoided asking Brett about Laikin. Until the last year or two after I learned about his new career and loved how much he'd become what he set out to be.

The weekend I left home, my parents blew up my phone, but I was over eighteen and could do as I pleased. In the beginning, being with Virgil felt like a dream. He introduced me to his parents, we traveled, and he proposed right after. I started looking at schools to get my degree in fashion.

Over time, I learned his true intentions, then I grew distant and planned my escape.

* * *

As soon as we finished dinner and cleaned up, I took Kayne home to rest on the air mattress, tucking him in. I wandered into the empty living room filled with boxes and scattered clothes. Laikin's tall figure leaned against the front door, both hands in his pockets. His heated dark brown eyes clashed with mine, and I released a sigh, ready to hear his thoughts on Virgil.

Too many emotions swirled within my head. "Say it." I battled with wanting to fight or take flight.

His nostrils flared, his deep scowl disappeared, and he stepped away from the door. Laikin knew his presence sent a tingle up my spine. "Place your anger at the right person, Amena."

"My anger? Laikin, I am not doing this with you." I headed back to my room to shower, and he captured my arm, pulling me back.

"Do like you always do and walk away from me." The harsh growl in his voice, I knew deep down, came from hurt.

In response to his grip, I pulled away. "Virgil was a mistake, but my son is not."

"Tell me why you walked away from me."

"Because—" My breath hitched, my stomach dropping in panic.

"Because what?"

I glanced up at him, and my throat tightened. "I wanted to get away from my parents but never meant to hurt you in the process."

"Not like you cared about me."

I craved every inch of him. Blatantly lying, like I never loved him, was ridiculous and childish.

When that car drove off that night I felt remorse, something in my gut said to turn around, but my head and heart never aligned. "Laikin, you were my first everything. How can you say I never cared?"

He raised a hand to slap his chest. "Because you allowed them to break our bond. You were my fucking everything," Laikin seethed, pointing to his heart. We started into each other's eyes feeling each other's pain.

"No amount of time could have stopped me from loving you, Laikin. I made a mistake and let myself get wrapped up in Virgil's words. I am no longer that naive twenty-year-old." Exhaustion poured through my veins. After the surprise visit, trying to work on my relationship with my family and raising my son was too much. I only wanted Kayne to be happy.

I watched my words pierce through him as he dragged a hand down the back of his head.

"*Mommy*," Kayne whined from the bedroom.

Hearing Kayne, I walked off and left Laikin there alone.

I peeked in on Kayne, the covers were off the bed, his little body curled up on the edge. I pulled the covers back up and left the door slightly ajar, coming back into the living room to find it empty. The entire day had been draining. I was starting to clean up when the doorbell rang.

"Who could that be?" I yanked open the door, smiling at Winter holding a bottle of wine. I moved to the side and shut it. "I forgot you were coming tonight."

Winter's brows squinted together. "What's wrong?"

"Girl, a lot. Please open that bottle."

I had paper cups until I had a chance to get the dishes sorted. Winter poured a full cup for us each, kicked off her shoes, placed her purse on the top of the island.

"Talk to me."

We headed to the balcony with the door open.

"Virgil came to try and take Kayne from me." I drank some of the red wine, staring up at the night stars.

"Babe, you should have called me or the police."

My body locked up with rage at Virgil going to these lengths to hurt me. "I know."

She rested her chin on her palm, looking over the city night life. "Is he trying to fight for custody?"

I yawned, rubbing my strained eyes. "Hell, no! He's using our son to get me back. He went to my parents' house."

"Virgil knows you're rebuilding your relationship with you parents."

Heavy silence filled our brief moment. "Exactly. The coldness in his eyes today told me I was right about leaving him."

"What did your parents say?"

Remembering the look of hurt in their eyes made me want to call and explain everything. "Guilt probably ate them up, but they were on my side for once."

"Well, that's good—I mean, not about the guilt."

I chuckled. "I know what you meant. Laikin was there and my brother."

Lines of smoke swirled in the air. A few young celebrities lived in the building and I'd learned they threw parties all the time.

"Brett and Laikin kick his ass?"

I swallowed the rest of the wine in my cup. "No, Virgil tried to snatch up Kayne, and Laikin blocked him."

"That's a good man, Savannah," Winter teased me a reference of the movie Waiting To Exhale, and I bumped her on the shoulder.

Tomorrow if we ran into each other, I had no clue what to say. "He is not my man."

A grin curled her lips. "Which is stupid,You both want each other."

"How do you know?"

"I can tell."

"He hates me." The words lingered in the air.

Winter stretched her arm around my shoulder and pulled me along with her to walk back in the condo. "Give him space."

"I just want our friendship back."

Winter grabbed the bottle to top off both cups, then gulped hers down. "Is my godson asleep?"

"Yes, he is and please don't wake him up."

If she had her wish, he would stay up all night playing, with her spoiling him. Winter had no kids—and no man, as far as I knew—so spending money and giving Kayne everything he wanted was her Godmotherly duty.

"All right, party pooper, let me get out of here and let you sleep."

"Thanks for coming over." We hugged each other, and I walked her out.

"Best friends are for venting and drinking," Winter said as she waved goodbye.

I watched her get on the elevator and leave. My eyes scanned Laikin's door out of curiosity and then I stepped back inside to shut and lock mine. Like I planned to do before she came, I headed to my bedroom to shower and go to bed, with thoughts of Laikin on my mind.

Chapter Seven

Laikin

A week had gone by since Amena and I had an argument and working closely together had not made it any better. The awkwardness started as soon as we got on the private jet to New York. Kayne wanted to come, but Amena promised him a trip in a few months. Amena and Sarai got in the car together continued talking and planning my schedule. Sincere blabbed on in my ear about his plans to meet up with an old flame.

"Laikin, you hear me?" Sincere called out, then tapped me on the shoulder.

* * *

"Come on, Laikin, are you scared?" Amena teased, throwing her bikini top on the side of the pool.

"Pepper, you got me breaking into the community center." Removing my t-shirt and shoes, I dove into the pool then pushed Amena's back against the edge with both hands planted on each side.

"Aww, my little baby is scared." Amena giggled and stretched both arms around my neck, kissing the side of my cheek.

"Keep playing and find out."

"My mom would kill me if she knew."

"How about we forget about our parents for the night?" A hand came up against my cheek.

"She wants me to go live with my uncle and aunt in Missouri." Amena rolled her eyes.

"You and your mother are just alike. That's the problem."

Amena nodded, her small frown curving into a smile. *"Kiss me."*

"Why?"

"Because you love me."

"Always, NaNa."

* * *

"Laikin!"

My mouth was bone dry. "Huh?"

"We're here." Sincere picked up his bag and I glanced around the plane as Sarai and Amena headed down the stairs. I unbuckled my seatbelt and stood, drinking the rest of the Jack Daniels. Lifting my duffle bag and checking for my phone and wallet, I strolled out of the plane to the blacked-out SUV.

"Sincere, I have you in the suite below Laikin. You both have the same private chef and security. Once we've rested, we head to the studio for the interview and then dinner later," Sarai announced, reading through the schedule and typing on her phone.

"What time do we have to be at the studio?"

"In four hours. Get as much rest as possible," Sarai demanded.

The driver pulled away from the airport, going to the hotel.

An hour later, I checked in and talked with my parents. I showered and ordered a meal, ready to relax and make plans for the evening. Hopefully, it wouldn't end up in the blogs.

Jumping at the sound of knocking and pounding on the door like the police, I marched into the entryway holding onto my towel. I was surprised that room service had gotten here so quickly.

"That's fast—"

Amena's hand fell as her eyes scanned my body. "Are you waiting on someone?"

"Yeah."

She looked away, scratched the tip of her nose like she used to do when she was nervous. "Who is she, another video model?" She chuckled.

"Is there a reason you're here?" My direct tone shut down her laughter. No woman has ever penetrated my heart. The way Amena had me doing any and everything for her from sunup to sundown. If she needed me, I came running. The second I learned of her and knew what she liked and disliked I made it a habit to make her days better. Whenever she got into a fight with her parents, she cried on my shoulder. Amena could tell me anything, so for her to have any type of jealousy of me entertaining someone baffled me.

"Sarai said it would be good to go through the outfit changes, and I figured since I have to check in with Kayne before he goes to sleep, it works better to do everything now."

"All right, come in."

"If it's a problem, I can get someone else." Amena hesitated, elevator dinging open as the waitstaff approached with my food.

"Give me a second." I ran to the bedroom and grabbed my wallet and robe, jogging back to pay the server. Amena still stood at the entrance of the room.

"I would rather have Sarai on my good side for this week. We can work together, Amena. No hard feelings on my end."

"Sure." Amena wheeled in two racks of clothes, then removed her iPad from her purse. I lifted the top off the food and popped a French fry into my mouth.

"You hungry?"

She scratched her nose. "No." Her stomach rumbled, and we both chuckled.

"Girl, come eat." I grabbed the bottle of ketchup to pour on my fries.

"Shut up, Laikin." She blushed, covering her face in both hands.

I mocked her tiny voice. "*Shut up, Laikin.*"

Balling up her fist, she punched me in the shoulder, but I barely felt the tap. "Ugh, you get on my nerves. Nothing has changed." Amena grabbed a plate and took fries and a salad with baked fish on top. We both took a seat on the couch and smiled at each other.

"Kayne's with your brother, right?"

Amena swallowed the bite of her food down. "Yep."

"He's a good kid. You're a great mom."

She held hand to her heart. "Thank you. I did something right in my life." For a change, it wasn't raining in New York. The sun shined brightly into my suite, against her soft skin.

"Is that how you really feel?" Amena had a lot of doubt in her young days, and me being a sounding board I tried to be there for her, but she needed to figure out on own how to navigate her choices—especially with her parents.

Amena shrugged her shoulders and sighed. "I'm probably the last person you want to hang with on this trip, Laikin, but I do appreciate you getting me the job."

"You're welcome," I said as we continued to eat.

"Sometimes, I used to wonder why I chose Virgil over you."

I tensed at her statement. When he tried to grab his kid, I was ready to put him on his ass, and Brett talked me down. I needed to stay out of it because of my career.

"My parents had an idea about us, but I never confirmed it. In their eyes, I became rebellious and they thought some boy was in my head. Only recently did I tell Brett." Amena laughed.

"Did he ever get physical with you?"

"A few times I thought it would go in that direction." Gulping down her drink, she ate another piece of her fish.

Turning my head, I stared off to the ESPN conversation on the upcoming race I had.

"I missed you," Amena whispered, caught my stare.

Scratching my cheek hesitantly, I wanted to say I missed her as well those first few months, but my ego wouldn't let up.

"Time is moving fast. We should go over the clothes for the interview before Sarai comes busting in here angry." Standing up, I drank the rest of my soda, wiped my hands on the napkin, and went to the bedroom to change clothes.

Amena approached, knocking on the bedroom door

seconds later, and I tossed the robe on the edge of the bed after slipping into sweats and a t-shirt.

"Try the black shirt and slacks for the interview." Amena held up both for me to try on.

"Thanks."

Amena stood off to the side and I strolled into the bathroom putting on the clothes. I came out to her smiling.

"I knew that was the right color."

"You have an eye for clothes." I winked as she came behind me, smoothing out the shirt and pants.

"Sarai will be downstairs in an hour. Try another outfit and let me take a picture before we finalize." Reaching for the next rack of shirts, she passed them to me to try on and we had several talks of what would work for each show.

I was feeling fresh after she got the outfits lined up. I got dressed and ready for the show. Sarai led everybody to the studio offices as paparazzi stood around, calling out names and snapping pictures.

"Laikin Trenton, is it true you and Callie are no longer engaged?" some photographer blurted out. Covering my eyes from the bright lights, I blocked the camera from my face and shoved my way through the crowd.

"Come on! We allegedly got you on a sex tape!" Another lie spewed in my direction.

"Fuck you!" I shouted and loud chatter erupted at my outburst.

"Laikin, let's go!" Sarai yelled, pushing me to keep walking as security yanked the passageway open for everyone to come inside.

"What were you thinking?" Sarai groaned, hurriedly typing on her phone.

"Shit. My bad, Sarai."

"My boy don't fuck around." Sincere's laughing annoyed me. Scanning the area, I saw Amena talking on her phone.

"Come on. We need to get the interview going." Sarai directed us down the hall, talking with the assistant to Maya West.

* * *

"Laikin, Sincere, so excited to talk with you both today. Normally, athletes of your caliber keep things under the radar." Maya charmed, sitting in her chair facing us both. Her sharp smile and piercing eyes would have any man emptying his bank account to make her wishes come true.

"Thank you for allowing us the chance to talk to your audience."

"Normally my husband keeps me updated on the latest sports news, but when I saw what you were doing with local charities, I told him I had to have you both here." Maya clasped her hands together.

"We appreciate the support." Sincere extended a hand to her, getting comfortable in the chair.

"To start it off, you both are single, correct?" We nodded our heads and laughed. "Had to let the ladies know," Maya teased.

"I'm single for sure," Sincere confirmed.

I gave her a 'keeping my mouth shut' look. "Very much keeping that private, Maya."

"Ooh, so we have a little exclusive here. I won't hold

that against you. My viewers and I want to know how Laikin started racing cars."

"Pretty much me falling in love with the speed, cars, and freedom of being in control of my own destiny. My dad loved taking me to monster truck races growing up, and working on cars got me into racing." I shrugged.

"Sincere, how about you?" Maya gave him direct eye contact.

"Kids don't follow my footsteps, but I was getting into a little trouble and got with the wrong crowd. Mom put me in after school program that went out on different trips and one was to Pierce Motors," Sincere confessed. I already knew about his past in and out of juvenile.

"A bad boy and playboy," Maya tittered, facing the camera.

People thought being interviewed and being in the spotlight brought wealth, women, and nonstop attention. Ultimately, I wanted my cars and the racetrack; that gave me peace.

"Before we go to the next break, Laikin, tell me about you and Callie. Social media has you two breaking up and getting engaged all in the same week."

"Gossip bloggers wanted to run a story and get an interview with me. I turned them down, and an associate of Callie's got money to fake a sex tape."

Maya flipped through her cards. "So, it's not true? The screen grabs online are fake."

"Yes. I do a lot of things, but leaving tapes around is not one of them."

"Weren't you and Callie off and on for a few years? And didn't you briefly have a relationship with a woman named Amena," Maya sprung on me in surprise. Biting the inside of my cheek, my eyes scanned around the set narrowing in on Sarai and Amena whispering back and forth.

"Amena is your stylist, correct?" Maya questioned.

As bad as I wanted to say fuck this interview, I had to be professional because Sarai is friends with Maya and her family. "She's a family friend."

"That you've dated in the past." Maya hammered in on my love life.

A showstopping smile dazzled me. Maya winked and smoothed her hair off her shoulder.

"Are we here to talk about all the women in my past or the future of racing?"

"We can do both. I mean, you're an eligible bachelor. The women want to know," Maya egged on.

Sarai rubbed her temple.

"No comment."

Maya laughed, gaze capturing Amena's. "Ladies, we hate to disappoint you, but I fear Laikin Trenton is off the market. We'll be right back," Maya announced.

The director yelled for a break, and I jumped up and stalked toward Sarai in fury.

"Calm down. I knew you would be pissed, but we had to work this angle before a blogger tried to run it. I got the photos taken down and sent the lawyer to handle Gossip Tea," Sarai rambled, filling me in before I exploded.

"Sarai, you know I hate blindsides."

"Which is why we had to put you on the spot and get Maya to air it in a way you wouldn't become a trending topic by leeches. Trust me, Laikin," Sarai said before going to Sincere.

I raked a hand down my face. "Shit." Even though I knew she was right, Kayne would be the one getting blowback if the media found out about him.

Was I protecting her son? I shook off the thought.

Amena came up beside me. "If you want me to leave, I will and I can provide you recommendations on another stylist. I'm sure—"

My glare held her gaze. "Amena, stop trying to run away. Sarai set this up to combat all the noise from the social media bloggers." I grimaced, hating that she wasn't acting like her old self around me. As the ex-wife of a politician, she probably had to field questions nonstop for years, but a high-profile athlete with a playboy reputation was another kind of obstacle.

"Maya's ready to continue. She's going to focus on the charity now and then we'll wrap up," Sarai let us know. I stomped over to the stage area, letting makeup do touchups. Maya sat down and put on a Colgate smile.

"We are back with the two biggest names at Pierce Motors Inc., Sincere Pendelton and Laikin Trenton. We like to get to know the men behind the cars, and recently you helped raise funds for the community centers around the country, correct?"

"A dinner and auction featuring sports athletes," I responded.

"Sincere, a young woman won a date with you—and Laikin, an older couple received the chance to come to the track. What made this cause one of your passions?"

"I see myself in those kids, growing up in a single parent household, no mentors until I got to the program. The help I received changed my life." Sincere chucked his head up and rubbed his chin.

The rest of the interview continued on with a speed round of questions from our favorite music, celebrities we've met, to me stepping outside of the racing world and into a few acting roles. Amena and

Sarai stood off to the side talking with Maya after we finished laughing and joking. Silencing my phone from the millionth call from Callie, I blocked her from all social media and uploaded a picture of me and Sincere on stage together.

I posted on my social channels and comments flew rapidly to see our location. We got back to the hotel, and I chilled, smoking with Sincere in my suite and watching the playoffs until dinner. I lifted my phone from the table, a flash of temptation had me feeling guilty for my thoughts.

Tisha: I haven't heard from you in a few weeks.
Me: Not much to talk about, we're good.
Tisha: So, call me when you're back in town.
Calliegirl: We can start over, Laikin.
Me: Callie I blocked you once, now you're turning into a stalker.

Sincere held out the lighter for my cigar. "What got your face ugly like that?"

"Fuck you, but it's Tisha and Callie texting me back-to-back.

"Shit, invite them over."

"Motherfucker, they're in California."

"Hell, I can do phone sex." Sincere shrugged.

"Get out."

Sincere burst into laughter. "Come on, bro."

"Nope, you would be the type to get me into some shit, and I'd end up with Sarai kicking my ass."

Calliegirl: Laikin, you know we're meant to be.
Tisha: I'm wearing your favorite thong.

Tisha sent an attachment. I licked my lips and shoved at Sincere, who was looking over my shoulder.

"Man, move." I tapped out of the thread and laid the phone on the couch, puffing on my cigar.

"Sarai should be down at the restaurant anyway. Fooling with you will have me on some husband and kids shit I had no plans of doing."

"According to who?"

"The way you protected your woman earlier I can see it in your eyes."

"Yeah, you smoking more than cigars if you think that shit." I put the cigar out, turned the TV off, then downed the rest of my Hennessy. I picked up my wallet and keys to lock up and left the suite.

Chapter Eight

Amena

Our last night in New York was a celebration of the guys making an impact with all the interviews before we headed back to California. Glasses clinked together around the table. According to Sarai, her company was looking good. It was one of the biggest public relations firms to have a twenty percent increase in brand awareness for their clients. Also, thanks to Sarai for tagging me in her posts, I had already lined up more clients, and my phone was ringing off the hook. The only downside was that more people were finding out about my past. After the last interview for "Morning Rise America" with Laikin, Mom called, saying how news stations were camped outside their home.

"For sure, give it up for Sarai and her team for blessing us with a kick ass stylist." Sincere was the biggest flirt and jokester, never took anything serious, and getting under Laikin's skin was his mission by bringing me up.

"Sincere, don't make me kick your ass," Laikin growled, gulping down his cognac.

Sarai giggled and I shook my head, ignoring him.

Twirling the pasta around my fork, I slipped the food into my mouth, feeling all the flavors sparkle against my tongue.

Dining in a five-star restaurant, while fans lined up outside waiting for pictures, reminded me of the life I could have if I stayed married to Virgil. I couldn't lie to myself and say Laikin was just as high profile as Virgil. Even though we had history, some parts weren't all bad. He'd been able to look out for me even when I tried to refuse his help.

Sarai drank the rest of her wine. "Amena, so many people are wanting your information. I can see you as the top stylist to the biggest celebrities."

"Already got endorsement deals wanting me to sign once I get back to town. That means you'll be needed ASAP, sis," Sincere said, and Laikin toasted to his comment.

"Laikin, soon as we get back home, the announcement of your deal extension is happening. Are you prepared for even more eyes on your life as the face of Pierce Motors and the responsibilities of cutting out the bullshit with Callie?" Sarai asked.

The waitress brought her dessert, and I declined with a wave of my hand.

"Callie is not on my radar. As soon as we get back, I'm focused on my career." Laikin sat forward, elbow on the table.

"Man, I'm ready to hit the club," Sincere said, rubbing his hands together.

Laikin agreed, slapping hands with Sincere. "I'm down." A few fans approached our table, and Laikin signed a few autographs.

Sarai peered at them both. "No." Their dynamic was hilarious.

"Amena can come along as the chaperone." Sincere's mischievous grin gave away his thoughts.

The sheer idea of being around them both with women scrambling for attention was not appealing. "No way. I'm tired and need to check on my baby."

"Come on, man, you have to celebrate, and Sarai will come out if you're there." Sincere tried to convince me to go.

"He is right about that," Sarai responded.

My eyes widened in surprise.

"Right, Laikin?" Sincere asked.

Laikin shrugged. "She's grown."

I pushed my hair back over my shoulder and agreed to hang with them for a few more minutes, but if anything got out of hand, then I would immediately turn around and go back to the hotel.

Laikin signed an autograph for the rosy cheeked waitress and pulled out his wallet to pay.

"Dinner's on the house, Mr. Laikin. The owner's a big fan," she said.

Everyone left a generous tip and stood. As I grabbed my purse, my phone lit up, and my brother's name scrolled across the screen.

"Hello." As soon as I answered, a strong hand pressed against my lower back. I stiffened and turned to see Laikin behind me. Our eyes locked for a split second. His chivalry was still there as he held the door open, allowing me to walk out first into the hallway of the hotel.

"Kayne wanted to say goodnight before he goes to bed," Brett said. I heard rustling through the phone at the same time flashes of light beamed in front of our faces.

"Laikin and Sincere over here!" Loud screams of fans distracted the mob of photographers. Sarai strolled to the black SUV. Instinctively on guard, like a pit bull in a ring, Laikin blocked anyone from touching me.

I scrambled behind Sarai, climbing in closer to the window. "Hi, baby boy."

"Hi, Mommy." Kayne yawned through the phone.

"Did you have a good day with your uncle Brett?"

Laikin swiped away on his cell phone with a brow raised and a crooked smile on his face.

"Yes, when are you coming home?"

"Tomorrow and we'll have the entire day to spend doing whatever you like."

"Yay! Can Laikin come?"

The torment of his presence every time Kayne wanted to hang with him was becoming too tempting. Hearing the loud scream of his name, Laikin gazed at me with a smirk.

"Um, I'm not sure, baby. Laikin has to work."

Kayne responded, "Okay."

"Listen, Mommy has to go. See you tomorrow. Be a good boy." The impulse to reach out and smack the smirk off Laikin's face rose.

Kayne replied, "Bye, Mommy."

I tucked my phone away after setting it on do not disturb, ignoring the stare from Laikin while the car pulled off into traffic. Making our way to club didn't take long. Sincere helped me out this time as the driver helped Sarai on the other side.

We walked in to loud cheers of Laikin and Sincere's names. A loud beat of music passed through the club as the women did their best to get to them. Laikin held on tight to my hand, which I never asked him to take. I wanted to yank it away to not give the wrong impression, but he insisted on me being close to him like this was my first time in a club. I went out with my girls back home plenty of times. Laikin stopped to talk with another guy, while Sincere hugged a woman who could barely cover her breasts in the tube top she was wearing.

"We have a section for you, bro." The owner motioned for us to follow him. Security created a space for us so we could get through the crowd from the bar to where we'd be sitting.

"In the house tonight is Sincere Pendleton, and our boy, Laikin Trenton, from the top league of drivers in the Formula One industry." Removing my hand from Laikin's, I took a seat. I grabbed the champagne bottle and glass, then poured a sip to calm my nerves after being in the public eye. If Winter could see me right now, she'd be ready to twerk and rock her hips in a celebration.

"Anything else you need, let me know, cuz," the manager explained.

I eyed Laikin for staring at me. "What?" My senses throbbed with the strength, feel, and scent of him.

Laikin spread his legs wide, showcasing his thick penis, which could not be avoided under his black slacks. "Nothing."

My back pressed against the seat. "Trip has gone well. Are you excited to get back on the track?"

Laikin gripped the bottle of Don Julio as the waitress placed more napkins on the table.

"Yeah, time to get back on to show folks who I am," Laikin boasted, lighting a cigar.

I leaned in close to speak over the loud music. "Since when do you smoke cigars?"

"A lot about me you have missed, Amena." Laikin sat

back on the couch, head falling back as he looked up at the ceiling, blowing out smoke with an arm stretched behind me.

Sincere waved a few women into our section and I knew the night would get even crazier by the thirst in their eyes.

"I see." Feeling more comfortable with our conversation, I turned to face him.

Laikin's eyes pierced mine. "Kayne good?"

I was grateful that he liked to keep up with my baby's shenanigans. "You heard him." I chewed on my bottom lip, crossed my leg, and took another sip of my drink.

Laikin chuckled, finished off his drink. "He's a good kid."

"Thanks."

A few more bottles came around, and we held each other's eyes. At the sound of a whiny voice, we both faced forward. "Laikin." Callie stood with a hand on her hip.

Laikin shook his head and blew out smoke. "Callie, what the fuck are you doing here?"

Callie acted like I did at sixteen trying to get Laikin's attention. "No, the better question is why are you avoiding my calls?"

"Yo, Callie, my boy is not interested. He got a wife already." Sincere winked at me, causing Laikin to laugh.

Callie frowned. "Who is this bitch?"

"Girl, the desperation is too much. Have some respect for yourself." I scooted forward, reaching for the bottle of Ace and pouring another glass. Laikin snatched it out of my hands.

"Hey!" I snapped. The tingling effects of the contact spread through me like wildfire.

"You've had enough," Laikin said, and me being me, I challenged him.

"You're not my daddy."

Laikin licked his lips, stretched a hand out to grab my drink as I gulped it down, and had leaned in a few inches from my face when we both became drenched. Callie popped her hip to the side with a smirk.

Laikin started to get up, but I reached out a hand to stop him. If she got him worked up enough to get in a fight, she'd post it all over the socials, giving a full-on performance.

"No, there's too many people around and you've had enough coverage on *that* lately."

"*That*?! Bitch—" Callie's words cut off when security yanked her up. She struggled to get loose and screamed, "Laikin! You bastard!" She extended a hand to slap him, but security stopped her quickly.

Protectively, he stood close and put his arm around my waist, being this close brought back memories of our time when we dated in high school. Glancing at the time on my phone, I decided it was time to leave. Sarai would throw a fit about Callie pouring alcohol on us and trying to fight Laikin after sneaking in here. It would just be more problems.

"Sincere, we're out." Laikin held out a hand for me to take. Sincere bent over and whispered in the ear of one of the girls he was holding onto. She giggled.

"Right behind you, my boy." Sincere slapped her ass, she leaned into him and tongued kissed him down.

"Sarai's going to be pissed," I murmured, walking behind the bodyguards, down the stairs, and out of the club. It felt like there were more fans than before, which meant Callie probably called them up to make scene as they hurled questions at us and demanded to know if I broke up their relationship.

* * *

The flight home was quiet for the most part, with me sleeping on and off. I got up early to get my place fixed up with all new furniture, and Winter came over to hang. "I'm mad at you." Winter pouted, holding Kayne in her arms and tickling his stomach.

"Why?"

"You kept my godson away this long and I missed so many things."

"You're right, but I promise to make up for lost time." I scrolled through my iPad, putting clothes together for Laikin and a few other clients who I had meetings with in the upcoming week. Since being back home, my schedule had gotten more and more complicated, so I ended up getting an assistant to help manage and book clients for me. Virgil tried to call me once, wanting to talk about us, but to me his priority should have been his son. As soon as I passed the phone to Kayne, he hung up.

"Start by telling me what's up with Mr. Laikin."

"We're friends."

Winter let Kayne go and he ran over to his toys in the corner of the living room. My entire condo was decorated in black, red, and gold trim from the drapes to the couch and tables. My baby's room was decorated in his favorite toys of dinosaurs and wildlife. Winter crossed her legs and cupped her chin to watch me.

Winter had a unique quality of picking up on my bullshit. "Stop looking at me."

"Nope."

I rolled my eyes and put down my iPad to pull out the ingredients for the lunch I planned to make. "How are things at work?"

"Changing the subject won't stop me from asking about dreamboat Lakin Trenton."

A knock sounded, causing us both to turn toward the front door. I gestured for her to sit, and then went to answer it, with Kayne rushing in front of me and twisting the doorknob.

I clasped his shoulder, moved him to the side, and checked to see who it was. "Kayne, stand back." With a fresh line up and muscular arms wedged in the black t-shirt, Laikin wore that familiar musky cologne that left me distracted whenever he had something to tell me. Kayne tried to get in front of me. Laikin stood with his hands in his pockets.

Kayne jumped up excitedly. "Laikin!"

"Kanye, my boy." Laikin greeted him with a high five.

I peered down the hallway. It had to be a woman waiting on him if he looked this good. "What are you doing here?"

Since the almost-kiss, we hadn't talked beyond business dealings, and those were mostly through Sarai. She kept me updated on any gossip.

"I have some people coming down to visit the track before I race and thought Kayne would like to see the show," Laikin explained.

"Can I, Mommy? Please? I want to go." Kayne looked up at me with his lip poked out and hands clasped together begging.

I looked back at Winter behind me, and she pretended to be fanning herself. "Laikin, I have too much work to do."

"She can go!" Winter blurted out.

A sigh escaped my lips as I rolled my eyes.

"Yay!" Kayne cheered.

My plans for lunch were getting derailed. "Wait a minute." My brow hiked.

"I have a driver today and my folks will be there, plus Brett," Laikin added, playing every trick in the book to get me to agree.

"Winter, do you want to come?"

Standing to her full height, she picked up her things. "No, I have errands to run."

"Oh, now you have errands to run." I threw my hands in the air dramatically.

"Stop pouting." Winter pinched my cheek, bent down to hug Kayne, and sauntered out of my home, making gestures with her hand behind Laikin's back.

"Mommy, come on. We have to go." Kayne jumped up and down, then ran to grab his jacket and shoes. I had some things to clean up—along with the food I took out that needed to be put away.

"Give me a second." I ambled away, leaving him in the hallway, and went into the kitchen to put away the vegetables, shrimp, and rice. I rushed into the bathroom to check my hair and clean my face, then remembered it wasn't a date.

I swiped up my purse, keys, and cell, sliding my feet into my brand new boots. Laikin held both hands on Kayne's shoulders as I locked my place up. The rejection from Kayne not letting me hold his hand made me feel a certain way.

"Since when can't I hold your hand?"

"Mom, I'm a big boy now." Kayne planted his hand on his forehead in exasperation.

"Boy!"

Laikin and I both laughed at his dramatics of trying to be grown. Leaving the building, his driver stood off from the side of the passenger door, popping the unlock button to help us climb in, and I smiled at seeing a car seat in the back.

I whipped around to face him. "You have a car seat?"

He shrugged. "Brett was going to let me borrow his, but I figured it would be best since Kayne and I would be hanging out more. If that's cool with you."

Locking Kayne in the seat, I reached for my own seatbelt and nodded. "That's cool."

Laikin asked, "Kayne, you ready to get on the road?" Kayne held up both hands and pretended to steer a wheel, kicking his legs back and forth in glee. I reached over to tie his loose shoelace and wiped some of the donut stains from his cheek.

"Ready!" Kayne's joy blasted around the car and held our attention.

The sound of his cell phone going off brought me out of my trance of enjoyment that we were the only three that mattered in this moment and back to reality of him being *The Laikin Trenton*. I could tell something annoyed him, but he agreed to whatever the caller wanted as he hung up.

His grin washed away. "See you tomorrow," Laikin said, tossing his phone to the side.

For some reason, the look on his face mirrored the one I used to have with Virgil. "Trouble in paradise?"

Laikin raised the partition in the car for privacy. "My folks want Kayne to come over for dinner."

My nose scrunched up in shock. "For dinner."

"Same shock I had, but I told my mom to not get

attached too soon. At the gala, you showed her pictures of your son, and all she's talked about is her new grandson." Laikin rubbed the top of Kayne's head.

"But—"

He held up a hand to interrupt. "Either you want to hear my mom go on and on about why you left, or you can go to dinner and let her spend some time with him."

I folded my arms across my chest. "Fine."

"Stop pouting."

I leaned on the window. "I don't pout."

"Shit, you're more spoiled than Kayne," Laikin chuckled, picking up the other toy car and playing.

"Whatever, Laikin."

Our driver cut across the lane to get into traffic. A few construction workers were lined up for breaks. A busy afternoon in Los Angeles meant upcoming events were happening around the city for Saturday.

"How is business going?"

"Very well, actually. My next client is Marlowe Shepard. Cyra, who's married to her bodyguard hooked it up. When I got the call, I almost passed out because I thought I was being pranked." I tittered thinking back to when Cyra's publicist called me.

"She's big time, congrats."

"Thanks, for everything you've done." The car pulled up to the stadium, and my mouth fell open at the wide billboard of Laikin near the entrance with his helmet in his hand.

"No need to thank me. Come on, little man. Time to ride." Laikin unbuckled his seat belt and carried him out, putting him on the ground so he could walk, holding his hand and signing autographs with the other, not letting go. I felt a little out of place in my distressed jeans and light green blouse with a few paint stains.

I honestly felt like the third wheel as I followed behind watching women fawn over my son, auditioning to be stepmother of the year.

Stepmother, Laikin is not available.

Shaking those thoughts from my head, I stayed behind when a few photographers snapped photos, and Laikin gestured to security to keep them back.

"We're going to Malik's office first, and then I can have security escort you to the garage and seats. I have to get changed," Laikin said, leading us to the elevator for staff. Hearing my phone buzz, I lifted it up to see a text from Winter.

Winter: Having fun with Baby Daddy?
Me: He is not my baby daddy.
Winter: Might as well be since Virgil left the position open.
He can fill your tank, and I don't mean on a car.
Me: Shut up girl.
Winter: You are running hot. He can cool you down.
Me: Why are you like this? He and I are friends.
Winter: Lay the pipe!
Me: I am not dealing with you since you left me.
Winter: Sorry bestie, you needed a family day.
Me: We are friends.

I was so distracted by replying to Winter that I bumped into Laikin and almost fell when the elevator got full. Before I could tumble, he wrapped a hand around my waist and pulled me into him.

"Uh... my bad." I tried to ignore his hard body and sexy scent.

"Relax," Laikin whispered in my ear and the feel of his big hand squeezing my thigh sent a vibration to my pussy and I hoped no one could smell my arousal.

Kayne was completely in heaven after we stepped from the crowds and made it onto the main floor. I tucked my phone away, finally releasing my breath when Laikin loosened his grip. Not letting Kayne run off, I held on tight to his hand and let Laikin take the lead.

Chapter Nine

Laikin

That call from my mother wasn't only about Amena and Kayne coming to the house; I also had to hear about Callie still going online and lying about how I broke off an engagement to fall into a trap with Amena and becoming a stepfather to a bastard baby. When I first saw the post, I wanted to wring her neck, but Sarai demanded I leave it alone and let her handle Callie. One thing Callie loved was her career as a model, and Sarai had connections that went around the world. To hear that my mom got a call from Callie, yelling about how I ruined her career, and she should be ashamed about the son she raised, was the last straw. Sarai will only have so much power to hold me back from having a few cousins kick her ass.

Amena's small curves fit in my hands like a glove. When I had to keep her from falling down, I had a familiar feeling that I foolishly tried to forget. Subconsciously, I kept thinking about stroking her thigh like I used to.

The rambunctiousness of Kayne, who was excited to

be here, reminded me of my first time working on a car with my dad, learning the ins and outs. Our squad strolling over to Malik's office interrupted my moment of relaxation. Some people might be shocked to know I hadn't gone out to seek women while on the trip because my mind was in a state of denial that I wasn't truly over Amena.

"We won't be long." I pointed for my security to give me a few minutes and knocked on Malik's office.

"Yeah, it's open," Malik's boisterous voice belted through the walls. I let Kayne go forward next to his mom and saw the smirk on Malik's face and I knew he'd clown me about it later. He stood from his desk, came around to kisse Amena on the cheek, and high-five Kayne, then extended a hand to shake.

"What's up? Are you ready for today?" Malik stood with his hands folded. Kayne tried to climb in his chair, but Amena nudged him back.

"Man, you already know I am ready."

"Glad to hear. The Roxbury couple is here and ready for you in the conference room and I got the photographers waiting at the garage." Malik picked up two VIP badges off the desk.

"Soon as I get them taken care of, I can focus."

"Cool, they paid a lot of money, so make it eventful." Malik slapped me on the shoulder and Kayne stood off to the side, staring at the racing track model on the top of Malik's table in the corner.

"Amena, you still hanging with this maniac?" Malik teased.

She held a hand to her mouth to keep from laughing.

I flipped him off.

Amena and Malik cackled as we stepped out of the

office. Kayne ran to keep up. All of us made it to the conference room and I waved as I entered, coming in to greet the couple with a handshake.

"Mr. and Mrs. Roxbury, I'm glad you could come today."

"Thank you for having us. My husband is a big fan of the sport along with our grandson." The older Black couple motioned to a kid, probably no more than fourteen, sitting in a chair, wearing a hat and jacket with my number and name across the side.

"What's up, young man? How old are you?" I walked around the table holding out my fist to dap him up.

Their grandson took out his phone, snapping pictures. "You're Laikin Trenton?"

"I am... and your name?"

"Uh... what's my name again, Grandma?" Marlon held a perplexed frown. The entire room erupted in laughter at him.

"Marlon, his name is Marlon and normally he would talk you to death," Mrs. Roxbury joked, and removed her shades from her eyes.

"Yes, Marlon. I am really standing with Laikin, the star driver of Pierce Motors," Mr. Roxbury boasted.

Marlon ecstatically lunged forward with his arms around me for a hug. I chuckled, patting his back. Normally, I liked to keep boundaries with fans, but he was a kid and excited.

"Okay, Marlon, let the man go so we can start the tour," Mr. Roxbury remarked.

Marlon released me, and I gently shook his shoulder to calm him down.

"You're good kid, chill. I'm normal like you."

Marlon stood in awe. "Seriously?"

"Laikin, time to go." Malik rushed the meeting and escorted everyone to follow me out as security held the elevator doors.

The revving of the engines pulled everyone's attention to car #34 in the lineup, driven by Ledger Holloway. He'd signed on with the team a few months back. He already had endorsements and companies wanting to recruit him, but he loved being at Pierce Motors because we treated him like family. I strolled to the crowd surrounding him and held a hand up for Marlon and the rest to stay to the side of me to keep safe. Ledger hopped out with his helmet and gloves on. There was a camaraderie at Pierce Motors; some of us got together, kicking it outside of driving, which was where Ledger opened up to me about being new in the industry and the downside of fame. With Sarai taking him under her wings, he was welcomed with open arms and genuine support. The tight-knit community, the trust, and respect they showed him made Pierce Motors the perfect fit for Ledger. His eyes widened in surprise when he saw me.

"Motherfucking Laikin Trenton, tonight is the night." Ledger's green eyes peered over my shoulder. I followed the line of contact to Amena. He knew she was off-limits from the moment I told him I picked her up from the highway and she was permanently back in town.

"Eyes up here, asshole." I held two fingers up in front of my eyes and gestured from me to him.

He chuckled and slapped his hands, giving me a one arm hug. "Off-limits, I gotcha... but introduce me, because she is *fine*." Ledger wiggled a hand at her.

Amena simpered like something was funny, and I wanted to choke him and slap her on the ass for thinking it was cute to flirt in front of me. My chest tightened with a mix of jealousy and possessiveness as I watched Ledger's eyes linger on Amena.

Being that she's not my girl, I shook those thoughts away. "Ledger, this is Mr. and Mrs. Roxbury, and their grandson, Marlon. You remember me telling you about Amena and her son, Kayne?"

Ledger cupped Mrs. Roxbury's hand to kiss the back of it, then took Amena's hand, kissing both of her cheeks. Amena grinned, and I yanked her hand away. Everyone laughed.

"Stop playing, bro."

Ledger's hands raised in mock surrender. "I can't have new friends?"

As I waved my thumb toward Amena, I said, "Not this one."

"Stop being rude, Laikin," Amena hissed, making my blood boil.

"Laikin, time to get dressed!" one of the pit crew members named Assah yelled out, and I nodded.

"Marlon, come check out the car really quick before the show starts." I directed him and Kayne over to Ledger's car.

"This is so cool." Marlon poked his hand inside and touched the steering wheel.

"Nonstop rush and remember if you ever want to get involved in this industry, you have to practice and learn. Put in the hours like the rest of us on the field."

I peered up at the crowd of people walking to their seats, as more cars came out to line up.

"All right, time for me to get dressed. See you at the finish line." Malik escorted the family, Amena, and Kayne to the bleachers. I jogged back to the garage looking over my car with the team before I changed clothes.

An hour later, sweat trickled under my helmet and down my face. I gripped the wheel as the light was gearing to change. I raised my thumb up to show I was ready when the announcer came across the speaker.

"Ladies and gentlemen, start your engines!"

The countdown began after another driver came out of the pit. The flag dropped and I took off feeling the adrenaline of the speed creep up in mind. Ledger passed another car, picking up speed, and I pushed to another level, bypassing CD Enterprises, Kash's old team. Doing another lap, I captured the moment, as more drivers came in behind me. I crossed the finish line. I threw my car into park, climbed out the window, and lifted my arms in the air, screaming in joy at my newest achievement. I ran to the bleachers, removed my helmet and handed it to Kayne, and hugged my mom and dad.

"Congratulations, son!" Mom bent down and kissed me on the cheek.

"Another win for Laikin Trenton!" I heard over the speaker.

A slew of reporters approached me while I headed back to the garage. I signaled with my hand not now and shook hands with my team members.

"Nice win, man." A few clapped their hands. Ledger came up beside me, holding up a champagne bottle.

"One time for the champion." Ledger passed around cups and poured some for everybody.

"To Pierce Motors!" I yelled, gulping down the alcohol.

* * *

I arrived at my parents' home that I had bought with my very first check. It sat on an acre of land in Beverly Hills. It was a spiraling three-story, 10,000-square-foot mansion, with a ten-car garage. Kayne tried to run around throughout the house as we walked inside, but I held onto his arm.

"Slow down, little man."

Kayne looked up at me with his curious eyes. "I want to see the pool." Kayne stared off at the large backyard and swing set that my parents had installed years ago for when my little cousins visited.

I kicked off my shoes and Amena followed my steps, helping Kayne to do the same. My parents came in, still holding hands—even thirty years later.

"Amena, come help me in the kitchen." Mom took off her coat, linking her arm with Amena's. Kayne stood next to me, and I picked him up and strolled around to the couch, then sat him down, tickling his stomach.

Dad changed the channel. "Son, you looked good out there."

Kayne's laughter filled the room as I stopped tickling him. I took a seat next to him, head against the couch. The minute I got my start in the business my parents reluctantly retired. Mom being a librarian and Dad working for the city bus, he hesitated at first because he wanted to always provide for us. When he saw I had investments on top of being in the spotlight, it finally let him relax and enjoy himself and spend more time with Mom.

"Thanks, trying to get more wins under my belt to keep up that contract." I smirked.

"They'd be crazy to take you off now. What does Malik say?"

"Now that he's president, we're cool, no problems, but you know my personal life tends to influence my image."

He whistled, then it turned into a full-blown chuckle. "About that mess with Callie?"

"Yes sir, it's over."

"Hope so because if you want something serious with the one in there, you need to cut the mess out and be a man."

I groaned, picking up the *Men's Sports* magazine with my face on the cover. "Come on, old man."

Dad kicked up his foot recliner and laid back. "Act stupid if you want to. She's going to move on."

I stared down at Kayne. "We ain't together." Even though we'd only had a quick conversation in New York, my walls had come down a little with her. However, I still wanted to keep her at arm's length, so as not to take my focus off my career. Separate from being my first love, she was a friend.

"Says you. Based on your actions and that little boy wanting to be around you all the time."

Kayne climbed off the couch and I let him run to the kitchen with his mom.

"Am I crazy?"

Dad put the toothpick in his mouth, twisting it between two fingers. "Amena's a good girl. Even though you kept that relationship quiet, I could see the love you had for her in your eyes whenever she came around."

I threw a hand up and brushed it down my face. "Her ex came to town and tried to take her son."

"He's the mayor in Atlanta. Be careful."

"Careful is what *he* should be, because if he tries to fuck with her again, it's on." Now older, I had connections to get shit done if Virgil tried to take Kayne again.

Shaking his head, the smell of good food wafted in the air and my stomach growled. "Your mother worries about you, and now a new grandkid?"

I chuckled at his comment about a grandkid, which was hilarious because Amena and I weren't a couple, but I would always look after Kayne—no matter if she's in my life or not.

"Chill on that grandkid label. We're working on being friends."

"Guys dinner is ready." Mom stepped in the living room with her hand on her hip and a goofy smile on her face. My dad stood up alongside me, reaching to hug my mom.

"Laikin, did you know Amena was such a good cook?" Mom nudged me on the arm, like it's supposed to impress me.

"Dad, tell your wife to stay out of my business."

Mom raised her hand to smack me on the back of the head. "Watch your mouth."

Amena and Kayne sat at the table. I took the seat on the opposite side of her to put Kayne in the middle, and Dad sat at his usual head of the table with Mom on his right.

Peeling the foil from the pasta, Mom scooped up each plate and passed them around. The only sounds were of utensils clinking and drinks getting filled.

"When's the next race?" Dad came to a few, but Mom hated to see me in that role because she worried I would get hurt.

"In a few weeks. That will determine if I can get to the finals."

"I used to be afraid of you getting hurt. Those cars drive so fast." Mom took a piece of bread and pasta.

"Honey, just like any other sport, they all have the good and bad to them," Dad remarked and winked at me.

"Amena, how is work going for you? Are your parents excited?" Yet again, my mom was trying to play detective.

Licking her plump lips, Amena smiled at me. "Busy. I picked up a lot of high-profile clients after working with Laikin."

"That's wonderful news, and Kayne's in daycare, correct?"

Kayne meshed some food together, and Amena rubbed the top of his head. "I'm a big boy." The entire table laughed at his outburst.

Kayne ate some more of the food, letting his mom wipe his face clean.

"I went to the house and filled the fridge—and found a housekeeper to get it cleaned up for you."

At the mention of my real place, Amena's face froze and her eyes narrowed. "You have a house?"

I was annoyed my mom blasted my business. I wasn't ready to move in until I had a wife and child, when I was less busy with my career. When we were young, I had imagined the house, kids, and life I would have with Amena, but now it was all just a faded memory.

As I kissed my teeth, I smiled. "Something like that."

"Something like that. Either it's a yes or no, Laikin. It's like you have a secret life."

"I do, one you would have been a part of if you stuck around."

All noise from utensils clanking on plates and talking ended. Amena dropped her fork on the table, scooted back in her chair, and lifted Kayne into her arms.

I stretched out a hand to block her from leaving the dining room. "What are you doing?"

"Leaving."

I was beyond frustrated with her anger, like I had done something to her when she was the one to leave me—on top of marrying Virgil. Yet, she was acting like I should just get over everything in one day. We'd established boundaries, better communication on how we got here, and now she wanted to throw a tantrum like she's sixteen again. "Amena, sit down."

Amena looked at my parents, placed Kayne on his feet, tossing her napkin on the table. "Mr. and Mrs. Trenton, thank you for dinner, but Kayne needs to get home and get ready for bed."

I stood to take them home.

Shaking her head left to right, she said, "I can find a ride home, Laikin."

Air stalled in my lungs. She was running again.

"Amena, I know you're upset, but let him take you home. I would feel better with it being so dark out," Mom said, giving her a soft smile of comfort after giving out the details of my house.

Amena nodded, then turned to stroll out of the room, telling my parents goodnight. I composed my temper and marched out, holding my cell. I let them walk in front of me, praying that we wouldn't have a blow-out in front of her son. Our driver jumped out of the front seat to open the door for Kayne, and I held the other door for Amena. She rolled her eyes.

We arrived at our condos a few minutes later, and I let my driver go for the rest of the night. I picked up a sleeping Kayne and held him in my arms.

Amena cupped Kayne's foot. I grabbed her left hand with him on my right side, not letting her tantrum run on any longer, and strolled into the building. "I can take him."

We made it inside. The ding from the elevator doors opening helped alleviate the tension. A dressed-up couple came out.

As soon as we made it onto our floor, she rushed to get her keys out and get inside, with half her body blocking me from following her in. I accepted the glaring anger that poured from her eyes.

Amena stretched her hands forward to take Kayne. "Thanks for dinner and for letting Kayne see the race," she mumbled and then shifted her weight.

"You might as well take that chip off your shoulder and let me inside."

"Laikin, it's late, and Kayne has daycare tomorrow." The fear in her voice stretched.

"Amena."

She looked me in the eye, moving to the side with the door wide open. I stalked down the hall to his bedroom, placed him in bed, and removed his shoes. I tucked him under the covers. Hearing running water, I came into the kitchen and saw that she had a tea kettle on the stove.

I leaned against the counter next to the island. "Say what you have to say and we're leaving it in the past." Overreacting to something dealing with me was her motto. I had to handle her with kid gloves at times.

Her shoulders hunched with a long sigh. "I...I can't believe you stuck to our dream." Amena glanced over her shoulder.

"I did."

"Why don't you hate me? I hate myself," she said on a sob.

I pulled her into my arms, brushing a hand down her

back, and swallowed the sudden lump in my throat. "Hate would be admitting that it was over."

Slowly, her head lifted up and she stared at me. "What are you saying?"

"We are the only ones who can write our story, Pepper. My love for you never stopped, even with you marrying someone else. That was a journey you needed, but your home is here." Taking her hand, I placed it on my chest.

"I never stopped loving you either, Laikin."

"Come here."

Our mouths touched instantly, getting familiar with each other again, before her arms went around my neck, pressing her body into mine.

"Mmmm..."

I bent at the knees and raised her up, her legs wrapped around my waist. I walked us back toward her bedroom. I kicked the door shut, put her on the bed, ripped off her top, and kicked off my shoes. She unbuckled my belt. I pushed her flat on her back, crawled on the bed kissing up her thigh, stomach, and squeezing each breast. Amena shoved her hand into my boxers, removing my dick through the slit.

"Laikin... please fuck me." Amena moaned, arching off the bed.

I captured her lips, spread her legs wide, and pushed forward into her entrance. We both moaned in pleasure at our connection. I needed her right away; eating her pussy would come later.

Peppering kisses up and down her neck and across her shoulder, I said to her, "Some things never change."

Amena lifted her head to stare at me, surrendering to the weight of my body on top of hers. All the air expelled from my lungs in one wild gasp when I got even deeper.

"Please...Laik—" Amena's lips formed a circle. Stretching her hands onto the back of my head, she buried her head into the crock of my neck.

"We have years to make up for tonight, baby." Both of us seemed to be in the process of rediscovery, sharing the same faults of being young and dumb at love.

Picking her head up, she blinked, caressing my cheek. Nothing else mattered beyond the two of us in that moment. I let my guard down and her walls broke as we both were determined to capture our memories from the missed time together.

Chapter Ten

Amena

The way he made my body feel replayed over and over, like our first time when I was seventeen. Laikin brought me to the cliff each and every time, reminding me of how our friendship turned into more, giving me a piece of his heart. His strokes slowed as he grabbed both of my legs, turned me onto my stomach, and slid a hand up my back. I spread my hands under the pillows, shivering from his touch. I felt like I was a puzzle piece he was putting together. I was powerless to resist him. Tears pooled into my eyes at what I did to us. A delicious shudder shot through my body when the tip of his dick touched my entrance. A wild need passed between us. The nibble on my ear, the warmth of his breath, and the moaning let me know this was home. I turned my head for an urgent kiss, sticking my tongue out. He sucked and nibbled savagely on my breast.

"I hate that I put us in this position for so long."

His mouth wandered up the tingling cord of my neck. "I'm willing to let the past go, baby. Just say you're home."

Laikin pulled back, pushed in deeper, and groaned. Unable to answer, I nodded.

"Come with me, Pepper." He moved against me, fanning the sparks of arousal, surging to the highest level.

At his soft touch, I trembled. "To our place," I whispered.

"Come with me and never let go, Amena. I never stopped loving you."

What we shared was more than love. It was beyond friendship. We were made for each other in this life and after.

"Yes... I'm coming." It was pure agony of passion, years of despair coming through.

Laikin became more possessive, slapping my ass, gripping the back of my neck, stroking faster and faster. Unable to hold it any longer, I came all over my bed. "Mmm... Laikin, I love you!" I screamed. He released right behind me, then fell on top of me, breathing hard and rubbing up and down my body.

Both hands made a heated path along my stomach up my breasts.

"I love you, Pepper." He rolled to the side and pulled me into his arms. He kissed me on the lips and lifted me on top of him. "I need more."

I smiled. "Making up for lost time? You're going to make me too tired for work."

"Good dick will do that to you."

Laying propped against the pillows, he watched me. Grinning, he ran a hand up my thigh, squeezed, then brought his mouth to my right breast. Love rested in his eyes. A hunger I remembered as the pleasures pulsed in my veins as happiness filled me. No longer did I have to be afraid of what the future held for Kayne and me. After the initial shock of seeing Laikin again on the road, after escaping a terrible situation, I stiffened in shock all over again now, seeing him like this for the first time in years.

"I missed your kisses, your arms..."

Moving down lower, I opened my mouth and licked his tip, moaning at the smooth taste. Laikin's stomach caved and he closed his eyes for a brief moment. I flattened my tongue, sucked him to the base, then pulled back and popped him out of my mouth.

"Don't stop." Laikin got harder, and lust danced in his eyes.

I wrapped both hands around him, twisted from left to right, spat on the tip, and kept him on edge, pressing him against my lips and teasing him.

"Amena, fuck...stop playing with me."

Playing my own games, I took him back down my throat. My nails penetrated his skin and raked down his thighs slowly. I closed my eyes. His hands massaged my hair and kept me at the pace he liked, exposing his lean, muscular body that he kept fit.

"My dick belongs to you, Amena. I promise." He groaned as I eased him from my mouth.

"My pussy belongs to you." Sliding down on his shaft, we both moaned as our skin slapped against each other, the sound ringing throughout the room. I was glad my room was far away from Kayne's, but just in case, I had already locked the doors.

We smashed our lips together as I rolled my hips, fucking him for the rest of the night. With a fevered groan and steady thrusts, explosions of ecstasy fell around us.

* * *

Weeks had passed since our first night having sex. No matter where he was, or what was happening, Laikin was on a mission to not be away from me for more than three days. He'd fly me out if he had to travel or schedule his trips around my work schedule. Kayne enjoyed playing video games or going out for a boys' night with him and his uncle. I wasn't allowed to go because they did man things like laser tag and basketball, which I beat both their asses in a few times.

While listening to my client describe her upcoming movie PR tour over the phone, I had some clothes pulled at the studio suite I rented for meetings. My name traveled fast, and I was booked up for the next six months. I secured space to see clients in person, and I was booked for virtual meetings.

"I need a total of ten outfits, and I need something for a celebration party that my husband is planning."

I held up the pieces. "Okay, so I am thinking we do a mixture of fun, flirty dresses for the morning interviews. Based on the schedule your assistant sent, you have four interviews in one day. I think wearing the crop top and wide skirt could work for on-air live shows."

Marlowe smiled in the FaceTime camera. "I love that idea, Amena. You're the best! Send me each look, and I will be in town to try everything on in two weeks." Marlowe cheered with a hand up in the air.

"Give me until the end of the day and I will have all the looks pulled."

Marlowe tucked a lock of hair behind her ear. "Thank you again for taking me on last minute."

"I should be thanking *you*. Everybody is buzzing about your work in the limited series—and there's even talk of you being nominated for an Emmy. If everything works out, we'll both have our names talked about."

Marlowe blushed. "Speak it into existence."

The knocks at my door caught my attention. I held a finger up at the camera for Marlowe to hold on, and I ambled over to look through the peephole. I smiled pleasantly at my best friend holding bags of food.

"Marlowe, let me call you back." I unlocked the top, letting Winter step inside, tapping to end the call as Marlowe hung up her line.

"I smell something good."

Winter placed the bag on the coffee table. "Honey, your man said to make sure you're fed and to take a break."

"You talked to Laikin?"

"I talked to Kayne and Laikin was in the background with your brother."

Chuckling, Winter opened one bag and shoved the other toward me. I picked out a box of fries, salad, and teriyaki vegetables. "Kayne is addicted to hanging with them."

"He's so sweet, he makes me want one. Then I think about changing diapers." Winter shivered, scrunching up her face.

"Girl, hush. I just imagine you having a nanny for changing the diapers."

"Right about that part. How's work going?" Winter took a seat on the L-shaped couch near the window. I went to sit behind my desk, took out the packets of ketchup, poured them on my fries, and placed my napkin on my lap. "Work is busy. When you knocked, I was on the line with Marlowe Shepherd."

"She's my favorite actress. Can you get me a picture and an autograph?"

"I can't promise that. You know my clients hate being bothered when they come here. I sign NDAs and tight contracts."

Winter drew her drink to her lips. "I can accidently bump into her." She sank back in her seat and released a burp.

"Well, she's my next biggest client after Laikin, so I have to make a good impression."

"Laikin has faith in you, Amena. Stop worrying. You already have your name in magazines and on the blogs as the top stylist in the business."

I slammed my drink on the desk and rolled my eyes. "Bloggers." Greed had come awfully heavy to some people these days; they would sell their own family for fame.

"They're good for some things."

"Laikin tells me to ignore the crap they write, but it's hard when I know Kayne will grow up and read some of that mess."

Winter tipped her head in my direction. "He had to deal with Virgil as his father. I promise whatever they write about you and Laikin will be a cupcake. Speaking of Virgil, has he contacted you?"

"No, last time we talked was about a month ago."

"You look much happier not dealing with him."

"His family probably has him on a short leash to focus on his campaign for senator and to leave me alone."

"I still can't believe he tried to take Kayne from you and that baby barely knows him."

Winter knew all about my struggles raising Kayne alone in my marriage to Virgil. One night, I had opened up to Laikin's mom and explained what happened, and she had encouraged me to talk with Laikin about those dark days.

* * *

"Mrs. Trenton, I really hate to put my burdens on Laikin."

"Child, when you're in a relationship, your partner is the one that gives you the space to release those burdens."

"Virgil was a mistake."

"We all grow from our mistakes. My son told me how you broke his little heart." Mrs. Trenton gently slapped me with the dish towel.

"Virgil's family has his whole life planned for him and tried to ruin mine at one point."

"You can't look at the past, only move forward. Your parents loved you even if you didn't think they did."

* * *

"Laikin has stepped up so much for Kayne. I feel guilty sometimes because he's not his responsibility."

"If Laikin wants to be in your life, Kayne will be a priority for him."

I sat back in my chair. "I can always count on you to keep it real with me." Laikin was soft, gentle, and so tender around me and Kayne. The world saw a bad boy racer who never took any responsibility, but we got that other side of him.

Winter flicked her wrist in the air. "I know being back in the spotlight is hard, but he's different than your ex. Comparing them will only lead to doubt and resentment.

123

Let Laikin love you." Winter commanded as she finished off her dessert.

"Speaking of love, any new dates or boy toys?"

"Same old, same old—drinks and boring conversations at dinner."

"Does my brother know about those boring conversations? I mean I'm still surprised you two hooked up."

Winter leaned her head against the back of the couch. "He does—and we are not exclusive. I mean he wants more, but I have to take things slow." The idea of them together gave me pause at first, me still getting used to them being flirty, but if he could handle me and Laikin, I had no right to give an opinion on their love life.

"Are you both seeing other people?"

She lifted her head off the couch. "Did he say he's seeing someone else?" Winter's brows crinkled together.

"Winter, you can't think he's going to sit around and wait on you," I scoffed.

"I need to get my life together."

"Yep." Both our heads swiveled to the left as my door pushed open and Kayne led the way inside. Laikin and Brett strolled in with wide smiles on their faces.

Kayne ran toward my open arms, falling into my lap. I bent down to lift him up, raining kisses all over his face. "Surprise, Mommy!"

"A nice surprise! Why didn't you call me?" I stared at Laikin as he bent down to kiss me on the lips. I wiped the residue of my lipstick from his mouth.

Brett walked over to the couch and sat next to Winter.

Laikin extended a hand to cup mine. "Kayne wanted to surprise you." The brightness in his eyes sparkled; it was clear he wanted to wrap up our little reunion and get me back to bed.

"Laikin, tell your girl that I can be here when Marlowe Shepherd comes! I won't harass her," Winter promised, amusement flickering in her eyes.

"When is she coming?" Laikin's long legs spread apart. His hands fell to his sides.

"In two weeks. She has a press run for her TV series." Kayne picked up my iPad. I changed it to a blank screen and let him pretend to draw.

"That's up to Marlowe." Laikin crossed his arms over his chest. His gaze flew between Winter and me.

"Boo! I can see she already got you agreeing with her," Winter teased, throwing her thumbs down.

Behind my baby's back, I flipped her off and she snorted. "Sis, how's business going?" Brett asked, ignoring Winter.

"Busy, since your friend here gave my business cards out." Despite trying to fight him on putting my name out there, I loved how generous he was. Laikin winked at me.

"I'm proud of you, sis," Brett expressed, taking an eggroll off Winter's plate. She slapped his hand.

"Mommy can I have pizza for dinner tonight?" Kayne asked.

I squeezed him tight, kissing his cheek. "I was planning on cooking, Kayne."

"Tonight, Kayne's staying with your brother," Laikin said.

My brows rose in surprise. "He is? When did this happen?"

"We have a date tonight," Laikin replied.

Deep confusion marked my face. We had fallen into a routine, and I figured we were past the dating stage. "A date?"

Laikin nodded, dipped his head down low, and whispered in my ear. "I plan on eating you for dinner."

"All right, none of that weird shit in front of me," my brother fussed, causing me and Winter me to laugh.

"How can you fuss at us when you're talking to Winter?"

"Winter's a friend," Brett stated. Winter raised her hand to the back of his head and slapped him.

Brett bellowed, "Aye!"

Kayne bent over holding his stomach in laughter.

"Little man, are you laughing at your uncle?" In a flash, Brett stood and stalked towards him, tickling his stomach.

"Laikin!" Kayne screamed in laughter.

"You're supposed to be on my side," Brett said.

"I am, Uncle B." Kayne pat him on the shoulder.

"How much longer are you going to be?" Laikin lifted his arm to check the time on his watch.

I logged out of my computer, putting my paperwork away. "I was wrapping up now, planned on working later at home because I have to organize some things for a client fitting." Laikin pulled my chair out for me to stand. He picked up my purse and bags from the shelf and handed them to me.

"Since you're wrapped up in your man, I guess we'll take a raincheck for the lounge," Winter explained.

"Winter, you know I hate clubs."

"Which is why we're going to a grown-up lounge to have a few drinks and chill with some nice, vibey music." Winter winked at me.

"How about you come for dinner?"

"Nope, I have a date I can't reschedule." Winter wiggled her shoulders. Brett glowered at her.

"Who do you have a date with?" Brett demanded. Grabbing my keys out of my hand, Laikin pulled me away from Winter and Brett's bickering, pressing in the alarm code to set before we walked out of my suite. They both had big personalities and constantly argued back and forth whenever they got together. Looking back , I could see how the energy they gave off was intense.

Kayne walked in front of us, and I gripped his hand while we stepped onto the elevator.

We headed to the grocery store to grab some things for dinner. Laikin stretched a hand around my waist, pulled me back into his chest, and kissed the back of my neck. Releasing my hand, we climbed out of the car, and I was glad Brett took Kayne with him, so we could have the night to ourselves.

"You should probably stay in the car."

"Why?"

"Because everybody is staring at us."

Two of the bag boys stopped talking as we approached the door of Publix. Laikin tilted his head up at them, causing both guys to reach into their pockets and grab their phones for a picture.

"This is why. I wanted to avoid the drama." I sighed, standing to the side as he took pictures with both. He came over to grip my hand then we walked in the store. I planned on making sea bass, baked sweet potatoes, steamed veggies, and my famous ice cream cookie sundae. Laikin kissed me on the cheek as I reached for a few more veggies and fruits. He kept his head down, staring at his phone.

"How was your day?"

"Good, I had a few meetings with my manager and agent."

"After your last win, they've kept you in the media." I lifted a bag of fries, shrimp, and grabbed Kayne's favorite grape juice. He moved closer to me, raised his phone, and took a picture of us together.

"Sarai and my agent have a few movie roles ready for me." Laikin slid his phone into his pants pocket and pulled me into his chest.

"Oh shit! You're Laikin Trenton," a girl walking with a group shouted.

"Time to go." I pushed the cart forward. Laikin chuckled and trailed me to the next aisle to pick up fish, then headed to the checkout line.

Within minutes, all the groceries had been unpacked. I started to prep the food while Laikin went to shower. Playing some slow jams, I silenced my phone for the night and texted to let my parents know Kayne was staying with Brett.

I swiped up the dish towel to clean my hands, then cut up more onions and poured everything in the skillet, cooking the veggies while the fish baked.

"Food smells good." Large hands wrapped around my waist as he nuzzled his nose against my neck.

"Babe, I need to shower the day away. Can you watch the food?" I turned my head, lips puckered together for a kiss.

"Shit, I can shower again. You can never be too clean, baby."

I paused in thought. "No."

He scoffed, releasing his grip, and I laughed.

"We will never eat if I let you shower with me."

Laikin pulled me back to his chest, pecking me on the back of the ear. "That's not true."

"Laikin, goodbye. Watch the food, please." I strolled

out of his arms. I went to the bedroom, grabbed a pair of shorts and a T-shirt, hopped in the shower, and washed my hair. Finally refreshed, I came out with my hair dried and pinned in a top knot. Smelling the food in the air, I came back into the kitchen to see the plates made up on the island, with two glasses of wine.

"Baby, you set up the food!"

"You cooked, so I set up our plates, and I will wash the dishes afterwards."

"I actually have the perfect boyfriend."

"Not perfect, but for you I will do anything. Take a seat."

Pulling the chair out I sat down, took the napkin and laid it on my lap, gripped the knife, and cut into my food. I moaned at the different flavors hitting my tongue, the sauce I used came from a recipe my mother taught me when I was younger.

"How are we going to navigate our dating life? Plus, Kayne—I don't want him in the spotlight, getting hounded by reporters at his daycare."

Laikin nodded in agreement and ate more of the steamed vegetables.

"At this point, fuck the reporters. No matter what I got you and Kayne."

"I appreciate you, but we both know they will pry into my background. You're already a high-profile athlete."

"Do you trust me to take care of your heart?" I let him rub the top of my palm on the table.

"I do."

"Then trust that any crazy shit written will get handled accordingly. I let the blogs run fake stories because it was only me, but I have you and Kayne to protect now."

"If it becomes too much, will you let me know?"

"What do you mean?"

I laced my hands together. "Virgil will end up seeing everything in the papers and will probably make some statements. Hell, his parents might even try to hurt your career."

"Virgil doesn't scare me."

"I'm glad you feel that way, but he's still my ex-husband, with a lot of pull."

"Fuck Virgil and let him try to come for you again."

Laikin pressed a kiss on my mouth, stood to take his empty plate to the sink, and started the water to clean. I ambled to the kitchen to stand next to him, bumping his shoulder. "Pinky swear." My eyes were fixed on him as I smiled.

Laikin turned to stand with his back against the counter. "Come here." Laikin pulled me into a hug, massaging circles around my back.

"The only way we work is by communicating, Pepper. Long as I have breath in my body you are not going anywhere. Let the media say what they want-- we know the truth."

I placed a hand on his chest. "Okay."

"Let's go to bed. I want to show you something."

"What do you have to show me?" I smirked as he took my hand, escorting me to the bedroom. Laikin took out his phone, typed in something, and waved it in my face. I glanced at his social profile and saw that the picture he'd taken of us earlier at the grocery store was posted, with a caption that said, *Me and my rider for life.*

"Laikin, you didn't." I grabbed the phone out of his

hand, seeing all the comments. Some saying congrats, and other people asking where the hell did I come from.

"Either they get in line or get left behind. My woman, my life." Laikin lifted my shirt over my head, while I continued to scroll through the comments.

"Let me guess @calliesexyone is your ex."

"Ignore her." Laikin unbuttoned my pants and slipped them down my hips.

"*Get with a real woman and not a pick me.*" I lifted my hands with air quotes.

"Baby, she's jealous."

"Obviously."

In the blink of an eye, Laikin turned his phone around, grabbed my hand, and placed it on his chest.He snapped a picture, and stepped away from me.

"Laikin, are you serious? I'm naked."

"Stop worrying, I only got your arm. I don't share, Pepper." He captured my lips, pulled back, and did something else with his phone and turned it off.

"What did you post?'

"Nothing. Slide backwards for me."

"I'm going to regret this tomorrow." I shook my head and spread my legs wide, getting comfortable on my back.

Chapter Eleven

Amena

The buzzing of my phone never stopped—not since the day Laikin posted us online with my hand on his naked chest. Something stirred up because they wouldn't let me be in peace, and it made me wonder if people really did not have a life other than making comments about other people's relationships. A few times when Winter and I went out, or I had Kayne with me, photographers swarmed us, running up to us and wanting to know if my son was really Laikin's. At first, I was pissed when they tried to spin it like I kept my child away from his birth father and was only looking for money. Then Sarai helped clean things up and had Laikin do a few interviews to shut the naysayers down. Virgil was the worst husband, but I would never deny Kayne was his son.

Today I had my client coming to do a fitting after a few weeks of delays. She'd been in and out of the state on business and other filming projects. The upcoming awards season was nearing so she had to be on point. My name would be heard throughout and would hopefully spark some more clients on my roster.

I shuffled a few pieces around on the rack and sauntered to the door, letting her inside.

"Hi, Marlowe. Was it hard to find my office"

"Not really. It's close to downtown LA. Being high up makes it even better." Marlowe removed her shades and opened her arms wide for a hug.

I moved to the side, motioning for her to come inside and take a seat. I already brought the rack of clothes to the middle of the room and lined up the ideas for pieces with the schedule of events on my iPad.

"These look amazing!" Marlowe expressed as her left hand fanned through the rack of designer outfits.

I took a deep breath, my heart racing. I had been wondering whether she would like what I had set out for her. "I have a few pieces for daytime and if you plan on going out at night."

"For those days, I will probably have a few dinner parties. My agent planned a celebration dinner if I win, but we should never get our hopes up," Marlowe joked.

Marlowe had become the biggest actress in the industry. A few people had named her the next Regina King. She'd taken on many diverse projects, from drama and action to comedy. Her latest TV miniseries on Starz had a lot of industry folks saying she would win an Emmy.

"Win or lose, a dinner sounds good."

"I didn't get a chance to ask if you can come with me —in case of a mishap."

I threaded a hand through my hair, thought about going on a press tour with her, but already knew that with Kayne's schedule and Laikin being busy we barely had time. Plus, I wouldn't want to put any distance between us when we just got back together.

"The offer sounds amazing, but being a single parent leaves me with little time."

"Oh, yeah. How old is he again?"

"He's three going on forty," I laughed.

Marlowe cackled at my response. I took a skirt and blouse off the rack and held them up for her to try on in the dressing room.

A knock at my door got our attention. "Oh, that's my friend. I invited her over. I hope you don't mind."

"No problem. Go ahead and try those on for me. I want to make sure the measurements work." Without checking the peephole, I twisted the doorknob... and found an unexpected guest.

"Well, I hope your taste is better than what you wore to the gala." Callie barged through, eyeing me with a calculated expression.

"What are you doing here?"

Callie planted her hands on her hips. "Marlowe is like a sister to me, and she asked for my opinion." While Callie crossed her arms over her chest, Marlowe emerged from the dressing room with a wide smile. It faded as she stared from Callie to me.

Marlowe inquired, "Is something wrong?"

"Ugh, no. What do you think of the pants and shirt?" I tugged on a silk blouse, which hung off the shoulder. I hated to lose her as a client because of her friend hating me over a man. Marlowe turned left to right in front of the wall mirror, from behind me I heard a snarky tone. "What Callie? Think it's too much?"

"My opinion is that you should find someone more

experienced with a big name and do all dresses, show off your figure and let them see the sexy you." Callie popped her lips.

"I don't know. I want them to see me as a lead actress with talent, not as a Hollywood puppet." Marlowe threw her hands up in the air.

"Wearing these cheap outfits won't work," Callie said with venom, pointing at the stack of clothes.

"Excuse me!" I snapped.

Marlowe stepped in between us. I tried to keep my cool and not stoop to Callie's level—she seemed like the type that would call the police and blogs to play victim. "Hold up. Callie, do you two know each other?"

"She's dating Laikin, my sloppy seconds." Callie smirked.

I had no intention of fighting, but she was pushing me. "Sloopy seconds yet you stay under his comments trying to get back with him, even though he blocked you from calling because you're acting like a stalker."

Marlowe gasped and held a hand to her chest.

"Bitch, you're lying!" Callie tried to reach around Marlowe with a balled fist to hit me.

Before it could connect, Marlowe shoved her back. "Are you seriously fighting over a man?" Marlowe spat.

Callie stood with her brows creased together. "You know Laikin and I have history."

"Laikin Trenton...Laikin." Marlowe's eyes rose wide in recognition.

At that moment, I was calm, but my pulse pounded with uncertainty. "Look, Marlowe, if my personal life is going to be a problem, I can recommend you to someone else."

"Please, if she has the same taste as you, we'll pass." In a condescending tone, Callie sighed.

Marlowe groaned and held a hand to her face.

"Girl, the delusion is real," I chuckled.

"No one is delusional besides you. Making a man raise someone else's child," Callie said, dragging my son into her lies.

"Okay, Callie, you're going too far now. Let me finish up here and call you later," Marlowe directed.

"You're taking her side?!" Callie barked.

"Marlowe—"

She held a hand up to stop me. "Callie, everybody knows Laikin has no interest in you. For you to even still go on about him when you both were just hookups for each other..." Marlowe spilled all her tea.

Callie's mouth opened and closed. She swallowed hard and stomped out of my office, slamming the door. Marlowe scrunched her brows and tilted her head to the side. "I apologize for my friend."

Taking another outfit from the rack, I passed it to her to put on. "No worries." The tension between began to fade.

"So, you're dating Laikin Trenton?"

Marlowe's steely gaze bore into my face.

"Something like that." I reached down to make notes on my iPad.

Marlowe pushed hair off her face. "The way you're blushing lets me know it's serious."

Picking up my phone, I prepared to take photos of Marlowe to keep for consistency and to know what outfit worked for each interview. "He's from my past."

The door opened and Marlowe came out with the short sleeve dress. "I apologize again for Callie's behavior.

I really want to work with you, Amena. Your dating life has nothing to do with business." Marlowe raised her hands up in the air, posing for the camera.

"Thanks. How does the dress feel? You comfortable?" I tugged on the end of the dress, reaching for a belt to go around her waist.

"Feels great, and with the gray heels and belt?" Marlowe gave me a thumbs up, after pointing at the shoes and belt.

"Perfect! Let's try the rest on, and I will have them steam-cleaned and packed to be delivered."

Marlowe grabbed the next skirt and shirt and went off to change. I had to make a reminder to keep my distance from her extended close friends before I really get on the blogs for bullshit.

***

The Beacon Lounge was lively tonight. I snapped my fingers and clapped my hands, listening to late nineties R&B from Tyrese and Jodeci. Winter forced me to come out after missing out on hanging with her the other day. Marlowe loved everything and she even recommended me to other actresses in her circle. Winter passed me a glass of cognac and I almost choked on the dark liquor.

Blue fluorescent lights shined around the walls, and mirrors captured every angle when someone got up to dance. "I like to stick to my lemon drops. This is too much."

Winter wore a cinnamon wool t-shirt dress. "Honey this will put hair on your chest," she tittered, then rocked her hips side to side.

I put the bottle down and picked up my martini.

"Something I don't need, ma'am." I watched a few women flirt at the bar.

As she released the smoke from her lips. "Mmmm...I needed tonight," she said, then snapped her fingers.

"What have you been up to or who?" I smirked, taking another sip.

Sighing, Winter hesitated before speaking. "Working and dealing with life."

I crossed my hands. "Laikin's ex busted into my styling session."

"Who?"

"That Callie chick."

Her brows pinched together in a frown, "The trick on the blogs constantly harassing him?"

"Yep. Apparently she's friends with Marlowe."

"Did Marlowe set you up? Please tell me if we need to call for backup." Winter cracked her knuckles.

"No need for backup—and Marlowe was sweet. She had no idea about the drama."

"Cool, I like her as an actress, but she can get it if she playing in your face." Winter playfully rolled her eyes.

I pushed her in the shoulder lightly. "Thank you for having my back, but we are grown, and I handled Callie."

"Happy you're being mature about Laikin and Callie. I'm honestly surprised you haven't confronted him."

"Maybe months back I would have been insecure, but I was the one that left him and married someone else. I can't blame him for everything."

Winter extended her arm around my shoulder. "Ahh, boo, you sound so mature. The old you was so spoiled, my god," Winter shrieked.

I ignored her comment and gulped the rest of my drink.

Winter took me by the hand, stood, and sauntered to the dance floor.

Either I was overly obsessed and dreaming or Laikin was inside the building. We hadn't spoken since the morning because were both busy with work, and now all of sudden my body had an intense craving for him. Winter rolled her hips. I followed her movements. Then the familiar, earthy musk of his cologne bloomed in the air. His large, smooth hands came down upon my waist. Kissing the side of my neck, we moved in sync, reminding me of how we moved in bed together.

I can be a bad girl for him.

He repeated the song lyrics to Usher in my ear.

Laikin raked a hand over my stomach and down my thigh. "Trying to take you home." Adrenaline pulsed through at feeling his dick again.

"I'm sure we can arrange that, Mr. Trenton."

"How much longer are you planning on staying out, Pepper?"

Moaning at the feel of his hand caressing my inner thigh, I turned to face him, throwing my arms around his neck.

"Surprised you haven't been noticed in here, but I can leave now." I ran my finger over his bottom lip. His dark piercing eyes sent chills down my spine, making my pussy thump.

"I know the owner. He made sure to let me in through the back and I have a hoodie on and shades." He patted his pocket.

When I looked around the dance floor, Winter wasn't there. I scanned our section and saw Brett whispering in her ear.

"Well, I thought it was going to be a girls' night, but

someone's already distracted." I waved at my bestie and brother in the corner.

Laikin looked at his best friend and chucked his head up in some silent communication.

He squeezed my ass, then pecked my lips.

"Let's go."

Most of the crowd had started to stare at him as we approached Winter and Brett. Winter embraced me and I grabbed my purse and phone. Laikin and Brett shook hands and made plans to meet up again. I cuddled up close with my head down, shielding my eyes from the flashing of cameras and phones as we left the club. I climbed into his passenger seat, fastened my seatbelt, and stretched over to unlock the driver's side.

"Kayne's knocked out at your parents' place. You coming home with me?" Laikin asked, placing his hand on my exposed thigh.

"One thing."

"What?"

"Callie came to my job." His eyes darkened, and his grip on the steering wheel tightened at the mention of his ex.

His lips pressed tight. "Shit."

"I handled her, but you should probably make it clear you and her are over." When we were younger, Laikin had gone back and forth with girls a few times, but now that we were back together and older, I didn't want to be like some feisty woman, claiming him to be "my man." We both knew that we're it for each other and no one could break our bond.

"Callie was cool and just a friend with benefits, but obviously she's taken it too seriously."

He stopped at the red light, extending a hand to cup my chin.

"After the charity foundation, I figured she got the message."

I interlocked our hands.

"Ignore her."

"Ever since you posted us online, people have gone crazier over you. They've googled and found my business. A few have even tried to book appointments.," I chuckled.

"Get your money, baby, but let me handle Callie."

"Okay."

Laikin arrived at a new location. I peered around the wide black iron gate to a large plot of land. "Where are we?"

"My place." Laikin typed in a code and the gate split apart.

"You have a mansion, the one your mom was talking about at dinner."

"You are the only person besides my family to come here."

"Seriously?"

He swerved up to the six-car garage and hit a button. The doors opened, and he pulled up. The doors closed behind us. I removed my seatbelt and gazed around the expansive area with multiple high-end luxury vehicles lined up, and a security system mounted on the wall that highlighted the entire front and back of the house.

"Laikin, I'm speechless."

"Come on, we can tour later." Laikin smashed his lips into mine.

"Mmm..."

I pulled back from the kiss, pushed the car door open,

then Laikin scooped me up in his arms, bridal style. He placed me on my feet as he unlocked the door and reset the alarm. The kitchen was all black with stainless steel appliances. There was a wide-open space that led into a game room with a massive TV hanging on the wall, a long, gray, soft padded modular couch, and a fireplace.

"These are all the colors I used to talk about when I was younger and wanted my own house." I turned to him.

"I hoped one day to have you here with me."

"Laikin." My eyes started to water at his sweet suggestion.

The magnet of our love couldn't keep us away from each other, and he raised a hand to tug me close and caressed my shoulder. My breath quickened at the feel of his lips leaving kisses along my cheek, behind my ear.

"I've waited so long, baby." Laikin grasped onto the hem of my dress, peeling it off and kicking to the side. I stroked a hand up and down his chest, then onto his stomach. I captured his lips in a sweet kiss.

Something in his manner soothed me. "Fuck me."

He growled and spun me around. He cupped my breasts in both hand and squeezed, then pushed another finger into my slick pussy, which only purred for him. The very air around him seemed electrified.

Biting my lip, I cried out, "Ahhhh... Laikin," and threw my head backwards.

A hum of satisfaction slipped from my lips. I pressed my ass closer, trying to be against his skin. Desire was thick, as I begged him to fuck me.

"Laikin, stop playing."

He covered my mouth with his thick full lips as my hands played with his soft beard. Our tongues slipped together, like it was the first time. I reached to remove his pants and shirt, taking control again.

"Bedroom, baby."

A familiar shiver of awareness of his lovemaking flickered through my mind. "Lead the way." I nibbled on his bottom lip.

The hallway held large art on both walls. A few pieces included his family. The three-story mansion with an elevator really made me see in him in a new light—of being a famous racer to the outside world. While we were growing up in humble beginnings, our worlds never seemed to come in contact with this type of money.

A gasp left my lips at the sight of his black, king size bed and the full desk and couch in the corner. The bedroom alone could be an apartment, from its large TV to its outside deck and walk-in his-and-hers closets.

"Lie down on your back."

Giving into his directions, I removed my thong and ambled over to the bed facing him. I patted the mattress, inviting him to come. His dark gaze told me that he would be calling the shots. His cheeks curved into a wide, admiring smile. Once he removed his shirt he climbed on the bed, picked up my right hand, and placed it on his curved dick, stroking it up and down. Ready to taste me, he removed my hand, bent to nuzzle his noise between my thighs, exploring me with his tongue.

"Ugh, yes."

I wanted to drown him in my taste. While working another hand to caress my breasts, I opened my legs wider, giving him room. He teased my nub and curved his finger to stroke deeper.

"I missed your tongue!" I shrieked.

His eyes were clamped shut, focused on my pleasure.

I blinked, feeling like bright spots were flying around me. His touch was firm and inviting as it traced the softness of my lips.

Smack!

"Ohhh, baby." All my thoughts spun out of control.

Smack!

My pussy tingled at the sting, and he followed the smack with a tender kiss. I felt like we'd been transported to another universe.

A raging beast of need was in his eyes. Lining up his dick at my opening, he kissed his way up my throat, pushing in slowly at the same time.

Powerful sensations built and throbbed below my waist. The force of his strokes moving faster and faster, my back rising off the bed. I felt like I was the race car that he was pushing to the finish line.

"Amena, I don't care what that other motherfucker thinks. You're my wife, and that previous relationship was a mistake." He groaned and sweat dripped from his brow. The headboard rattled.

He pulled out of me and flipped my body to the side. He thrusted forward, holding my hands together, pumping harder and harder. I made a low throaty sound of pleasure, eyes and mouth open at the intensity of his movements.

A scream of pleasure tore from my lips. "Laikin! Jesus! Oh please, baby, I want to come."

His body radiated a raw and primal strength. "Your pussy takes me so well, baby. This shit is biting really good. Fuck!" One hand slid around to caress my belly, then my nipple. I loved how he kissed every stretch mark and my little stomach, never letting me get in my head about the extra weight from pregnancy.

Together, we gasped, moaned, and writhed. Our skin slapped together, sounds filling the room.

Slap!

He smacked me on the ass.

"Come for me, Pepper." A tormented groan pierced my ears, and I shook underneath him, arching my back a little to catch the ripple of my ass against his stomach.

Letting my hands go, I scraped my nails against the sheets. He stiffened and convulsed; coming right behind me. Laikin's body trapped me , as his mouth possessed mine and trailed along my collarbone, down to my chest.

I was anxious to taste him, to take him into my mouth like last time. I was still amazed by his thickness. I gripped the base of his cock and turned him on his back, lowering my head. I made a fist around his thickness and began to lubricate with a mixture of my spit and precum at his tip.

Laikin's arm was thrown over his eyes, and he tensed at the first touch, making his arousal ignite again.

I flattened my tongue under the sensitive tip.

"Baby," he groaned, gazing at me.

I lingered on the tip for another few minutes, then moved my head up and down the hard length of his erection. His fingers knotted in my hair, working my head up and down at a pace he controlled.

"Shit."

"Mmmm..." I forced my throat to open wide for him, taking him deeper.

"Damn, Amena. Baby, keep going."

I popped him out of my mouth and licked both his balls while stroking his dick. He tightened his hand on my hair.

The warmth of his soft flesh was intoxicating. "I need my pussy, baby."

"She's wet for you." My body tingled under his touch.

"Come up here and let me taste her."

As I moved in to sixty-nine position on him, I licked up the pre-cum and took his long, curved dick in my mouth to suck him off, while he drank deep from my candid well of pleasure for the rest of night.

Chapter Twelve

Laikin

I was pulling up at the restaurant with Amena, who was sitting pretty, with her hair away from her face, showcasing the curve of her neck and her kissable lips. After getting blasted on social media at people thinking I was cheating on Callie, I made it clear we were never a couple. Amena's been the girl for me, even when we weren't together. The pictures, along with Sarai's statement of keeping my personal life private, only garnered more interest and even magazines wanted us to do joint interviews. I told her to decline, because nothing would get in the way of our relationship and that included her ex-husband. Thankfully, he'd stayed off our radar—even to the point of ignoring his son. For a grown man to not be responsible for his child, it only pissed me off more. Accepting Kayne wasn't hard because the kid was smart, funny, and loveable.

I helped Amena out of the car and set the alarm. I pushed through the crowd of fans who were noticing me and walked past them to the entryway of the restaurant. One of her favorite meals was Indian food, the spicier the better, and I had made a reservation for a private table in the back.The hostess gave a warm smile. I scanned the paintings on the walls, as the people around us murmured and talked. The robust smells of spices lingered in the air, while the waitresses rushed by to bring out orders.

I held up two fingers. "Two for Trenton reservation."

Our eyes locked and she checked off my name, taking menus and escorting us to section. I helped Amena take a seat then went to the other side of the table. It immediately became a surreal moment from a fleeting time that I thought would never happen again. A sense of weightlessness struck me to see her happy based on my actions.

Her hand glided over the table to engulf mine. "For the first time in months, I'm excited to be out on a date, like a real adult."

"We eat first, and then I have another surprise for you afterwards."

"What is it?"

Our waitress appeared, placed straws on the table and filled our glasses with water before pulling out her notepad.

"Hello, I will be your waitress tonight. My name is Sheila."

"Thank you, Sheila. What's most important is our continued privacy." I wanted to make sure our back table would be clear of me getting hounded. I could have called security, but my goal was to have an intimate dinner with Amena.

Shelia said, "No problem, Mr. Trenton. Can I start you with a drink?"

"I will take red wine," Amena ordered as she closed the menu.

"Same—and can we get the curry special, and the rista meatball dish?" I ordered for the both of us.

Sheila reached to take the menus from the table, thanked us, then sauntered off to the back.

Amena clasped her hands together, with her elbow on top of the table. "Are you going to keep the next stop a surprise for real?"

Instinct made me skate my hands out to grip the top of her hand. "Yes."

The sweet aroma of strawberries invaded my nose. "Fine, be a sorry sport." Amena's voice was low and stoic.

The wine glasses were placed on the table, and the bottle was left in a tub of ice to the side. I picked up my glass to make a toast. "To the future."

"To the future." We clinked glasses and Amena sipped on her wine.

"Virgil, Callie, and anyone else cannot make a difference in our lives, unless we choose to let them."

"You're right."

"I know I am."

Twenty minutes later, the food was delivered, and I scooped up my napkin and utensils to eat.

"So, you don't think it's too fast?"

"No, we're not kids anymore. I have plans for you and Kayne."

"Thank you for including him. I know dating someone with a kid can be hard. Probably don't tell you enough how much it means to me when you helped get us the condo."

"At first when you came around, I had doubts, but that changed."

Her eyes blinked rapidly in thought. "Same and I

really care about you, Laikin. To be honest, I never stopped loving you."

"Virgil and Callie are the past." I took a sip of my drink, prayed she understood my words. "What are you planning to do for his birthday?"

She was smiling and radiant. "A small party with family and a few friends."

"I can have Sarai help arrange the party."

"No, that's too much."

"Amena." For some reason I found her displeasure amusing.

She wagged her finger. "Laikin, her job is not to tend to your girlfriend."

"She's down to help me, and you're an extension of me."

Amena said through an awkward chuckle, "Sarai's going to kill you one day."

"I pay her more than enough to put up with me."

Dinner continued as we talked for the rest of the evening and we took our dessert to go. I paid the bill, helped her to the car, and sped off, avoiding another onslaught of fans that had gathered when we stepped out of the restaurant together.

Flying through the light traffic on main road finally pulled up to the K1 Speed Go-Kart Racing center. I turned off the ignition, and watched as her eyes moved from the building and back to me with her mouth wide open. I whipped around to the backseat and pulled out a pair of shoes for her to change into.

"Laikin," she breathlessly whispered, taking the shoes from me to switch.

Unlocking our doors, I came around to her side and held a hand for her to take. "Come on."

"You remembered our first date." Her wet tears slid down her cheek.

When her eyes sparkled, I grinned and grabbed the handle of the door. The night air was still cool to the touch.

"You owe me after you cheated me out of best of three."

Amena bounced on the balls of her feet. "That's a lie!" She shot me a side-eye.

"One drive and whoever wins is crowned the best."

My baby held up her pinky finger. "Deal."

"Must be real if you got the pink finger out." I smiled lopsidedly at her and a surge of excitement lit up her features.

After I paid, the desk staff showed us to our section.

"Wow, I hope your ego can handle being second-best," Amena teased, sticking out her tongue.

"Pepper, we both know I will dust your ass."

"Talk is cheap, playboy." Amena clapped me on the stomach and got situated in the go-kart with her helmet on.

"Stop talking and put your big girl panties on," I taunted with trash talking, and climbed into the kart. Getting the signal, we took off, and I watched both sides as I came around the corner of the track. Amena was right behind me. I tried to weave in and out to test her, and she did something that completely distracted me.

"Laikin, I can't wait to suck your dick."

My brain tapped out, and my dick got hard. I shook it off so I could catch up. She made the one lap and I finally came up alongside her to do another lap.

Amena knew she was a distraction. "I know that dick is ready for me."

It caused me to stop, and I looked in her direction. She was laughing as she pulled up to the finish line.

I bit my lip. "You cheated!"

She ignored me, jumping for joy because she won. I removed the helmet and stared down at her with lust in my eyes.

"Look at my dick." I knew the thought of her licking my tip would distract her.

Amena cleared her throat. She ran her fingers over my broad shoulders, and my arms snaked around her body.

"Be a good boy and I might let you play with the back of my throat."

My eyes darkened, and when I gripped her butt, her eyes sparkled with need. "One more round." I pecked her on the mouth.

The both of us broke into a smile.

"Fine, one more."

Every moment felt like old times-- carefree, like being kids again. I won the next two rounds, and we called it quits to go home and finish off the night by fucking and sucking to see who had the most orgasms.

* * *

Feeling a slight buzz from last night, I slowly removed my shades and relaxed in the chair across from Sarai in her office. I promised Amena that I would handle Kayne's birthday party and, after the extra shower sex we had when I woke up, my ass was all too happy to get over there in a hurry.

"Let me guess, you had a nice night with your girl." Sarai tore up a piece of paper and tossed it in the trash.

"Every moment with my girl is perfect."

"Get to the reason why you're barging in my office for my attention, Laikin. I'm still cleaning up the mess from you boasting on the race track other day."

"Why would I slack on my joy in winning a race? They better get thicker skin."

"Typical male driven ego."

"Sarai, you are my favorite."

"Which means you want something."

"Nothing too crazy."

"Answer is no."

"I didn't even tell you what I need help with. At least hear it first."

"Go ahead."

"Kayne's birthday."

Like a tornado she ripped my idea apart. "No."

"Sarai."

Her eyes flared up but cooled down. "Laikin, I am running a million-dollar business; you are not my only client."

"*Favorite* client—you can admit it."

A small part of her liked Amena. "Funny."

"Come on, sis. A small gathering of his friends and family, at Disneyland or something."

"Disneyland!"

"Too small?" I jested.

Sarai pointed at the door. "Laikin, get out of my office."

"Once you agree to handle the party planning, I will leave and not bother you for a week."

"That's a lie because we have a magazine interview coming up."

"All the more reason to help your brother out. I promised my girl."

"See, promising something you had no business even dreaming up... I am not an assistant. I help to keep your shenanigans out of the public eye."

I was loving every minute of getting under her skin. "And you do a beautiful job, sis."

"Get out!" Her glare was comical.

"Okay, I will pay you an extra Twenty thousand on top of your normal fee."

Sarai caressed her cheek. "An extra Twenty thousand on top of my fee? You love her."

I sighed. "Yes or no, Sarai."

"I hate to disappoint children. Make it thirty, and you got a deal."

"Damn, Sarai, you robbing your favorite client."

"No, I'm setting expectations that you will not drop shit on my lap last minute again without paying up, Mr. Trenton."

I rose out of the chair. "Here we go with the Mr. Trenton stuff again."

"Have Amena send the details, and when do you need the party?"

"A month."

"Seriously?"

I reached in my pocket to pull out my cell phone. "Keep me posted and the money is transferring right now."

"Bet your accountant hates you."

"She loves me more when bonuses drop every year."

My afternoon was relaxing. As soon as I left Sarai's, I picked up lunch for Amena and headed to her office. After parking, I pulled on a hoodie to avoid drawing the attention of the cameras. Her building has no security and there was a lot of traffic from the other businesses on the same floor as Amena's. I grabbed the food and headed inside. I knocked and heard heels clicking on the floor. She opened the door and a small smile greeted me.

"Brought you lunch."

"Thank you, babe. You shouldn't have." Amena stood to the side to allow me to enter.

I dropped the bag on the table, linked an arm around her waist, and pulled her on top of me as I laid on the couch, slipping a hand under her shirt.

"Oh..."

My girl was warm-hearted, sensible, and not with me for the money—even though I liked to spoil her.

"Love that sound, baby."

"What are you doing?"

"I missed you."

"Ah!" Amena gasped when my finger pressed against her pussy.

"Relax, you will have people thinking I'm killing you in here."

A look of bliss fell over her face. "Don't stop."

My finger dipped in and out, feeling her warmth embracing my intrusion.

"Oh God."

I gently bit her neck and soothed away the sting with my tongue as I could feel her clench around my fingers and her juices drip onto my pants.

"Fuck me."

I ran my hands through her hair and gripped it tight, ready to slide into her. I fed her my tongue, and Amena panted, clumsily fumbling with the strings on my joggers to pull my dick out. I was grateful that she was wearing a loose skirt today. I eased it around her hips, pushed her panties over, and helped her ease down onto my dick.

"Damn, baby."

"I have a client coming in ten minutes. You better hurry up."

The feel of her skin jolted my senses. "Shit, they're gonna have to reschedule."

"Stop playing, Laikin." Her skin glowed with a faint sheen.

"Fuck, Amena!"

I hated to rush, but her business was important to her, and I had plans to get in some practice later today. There were no more words, just sounds of passion. With every whisper, every moan, I made her mine.

"Now you got me all sweaty and my client is probably parking right now." Amena moved off me, pushed her skirt down, and slicked down her peach crinkled knit top.

All the furniture was modern, the carpet a shade of gray. The curtains were open, letting the sunlight stream along the walls.

I put myself back together, pinched my nose, and sat up straight. "One of the reasons I came here is because Sarai is on board with planning Kayne's birthday party."

Amena came out of the bathroom in her office, holding a wipe. "How much is the cost? I know she's in high demand."

"Cost doesn't matter."

"You're not paying." I hopped up and went to wash up.

Turning off the faucet I tossed the towel in the bin, and stared at her, then bent down and raised her chin. "Have a good day, and eat your lunch." I ignored her stare.

"We're not done talking about the party!"

I stalked out of the office, pressed a button for the

elevator, feeling my phone vibrate in my pocket. I lifted it out of my pocket right as the bell dinged, and I hopped on, returning a text to Sarai.

Sarai: What is the theme?
Me: He loves Spiderman.
Sarai: It's going to be a very expensive day for you.
Me: No budget, he can have whatever he wants.
Sarai: That's what I like to hear.
Me: Thanks Sarai. I appreciate you.
Sarai: You better.

I stepped out and headed to the parking structure and slid back in my vehicle, leaving my phone on the seat. I clasped the seatbelt, started the car and drove out of the building, hearing fire trucks. A bus rolled by when I came to a street light.

Speeding through the green light, I headed home to shower, work out, and prepare for the upcoming race.

Chapter Thirteen

Amena

A few weeks had passed since Laikin informed Sarai that he would be handling Kayne's birthday party, and deep down I was grateful, since my life had exploded with new clients. The only downside was him paying for the entire event. He refused to take any money from me.

I had Kayne up for an early doctor's appointment. He was not in the mood to be bothered and I had to bribe him with pancakes and ice cream. Laikin stayed at his condo last night. He'd worked late, making a few appearances, and me looking at designs all day left me exhausted. I held the door open for Kayne and he ran into the toy section and sat down with another kid. I stopped off at the reception desk and checked him in for the appointment. I sat down a few seats from him and picked up a magazine. A few babies cried, sending me back to when Kayne was that young.

"Ma'am?" the nurse called.

I tossed the magazine back on the table and stood up. "Yes?"

"Insurance no longer has you covered."

"Excuse me."

"Today will be out of pocket."

"But my son has full coverage." I reached into my purse to grab my insurance card.

"Unfortunately, it shows that you are no longer covered—along with Kayne."

"That bastard."

"Kayne!" The nurse came out and called his name before I could call Virgil. I put my phone back in my purse and wrangled Kayne to go in the back.

"Kayne, how are you doing today?" Doctor Ramisha pulled on her gloves and sat down in front of him.

"Hi, Doctor. Ramisha. I'm fine," Kayne replied.

"Love to hear you're doing good. Do you mind if I check your ears and tongue?" Doctor. Ramisha had been Kayne's doctor since we moved back. My parents recommended her because she's one of their close friends. The exam didn't take long, and he got a sucker, let my hand go, and skipped out of the room. Still feeling angry at Virgil, I helped Kayne get in the car and turned the air on, while I dialed Winter.

"Hello."

I checked to see if Kayne was paying attention before I spoke. "Winter."

"Hey, boo."

When I had my son, I let my anger go. They say children calm you down, and it was true, but right then, I had to count to ten to keep my anger at bay. "Tell me to calm down before I call Virgil."

"Calm down."

"Winter, he removed Kayne off his insurance."

"Virgil's always been a piece of shit. I told you that a long time ago."

I glanced back at Kayne playing with his toys. "I know, and it pisses me off. Virgil will go on in life, never knowing how special it is to raise Kayne."

"Where are you now?"

"In the parking lot of the doctor's office in Brentwood."

Winter reassured me. "Try to remember Virgil's going to get his payback one day."

"I need to call him."

"He's not worth a call. Laikin's in your life now."

I sometimes did wish that Kayne were his son. "Oh, about Laikin—that man decided to pay for Kayne's entire party."

Winter whistled through the phone. "Shit, he got a brother?"

"No, Winter. I'm serious."

"Girl, he wants to spoil you. I say go ahead and let Laikin spoil you. As far as Virgil, if you need to get a good read on him, then call and curse him out and block his number."

"Thanks, Winter."

"If you want to meet at your place later, I can bring food."

"Once I drop Kayne at daycare and handle some work, I'll call you."

"Talk soon, babe."

I stepped out of the car to speak with Virgil privately away from Kayne's ears. I clicked off and dialed Virgil's number, listening to the ringing tone. "Hi, Baby Boy." I put on a smile when Kayne waved at me from the car.

"What do you want, Amena?" Virgil grumbled over the phone.

I glanced and saw Kayne roll the window down. "Mommy! I go be late for school."

"One second, Kayne." I held my hand up in the air.

Virgil always managed to be a complete turnoff when he didn't get his way. "You made the decision to leave, so calling me now for money won't happen."

"Why did you take Kayne off your insurance? Me, I understand, but your son?"

"He's not my son."

"Virgil, I swear to god, you are a piece of shit and I regret ever meeting you."

"The feelings are mutual. You were good pussy, but I can buy that anywhere."

"Fuck you!"

He chuckled through the phone. "Figured you could keep getting a free ride, and I would just move on? Bitch, you cost me some business."

"If you acted more like a husband and father, and if you were there when I gave birth to your son, then I might have loved you. All you cared about was your career."

"My family never wanted me to marry you. I should have listened, but I thought you were the one."

I sucked my teeth. "You are joke. The moment you proposed your mom gave me the death stare. She did everything in her power to make you hate me."

"And she was right."

My stomach tightened at the rejection.

I gasped. "You know what? I have officially grown out of my hatred. Kayne has a father figure in his life who loves him."

"My rights will be signed over. Don't call me again."

Virgil disconnected the line, and I tossed the phone in my bag, and hopped in the car to leave.

The love of my son was the most important thing to me. Virgil would regret it one day when he was on his deathbed, looking back on his life, missing out on Kayne's moments. The way he portrayed how our love would be my saving grace should have been the red flag, but I continued to buy into the lies. Laikin was more of a father to Kayne. He didn't even blink once he heard about the birthday party, and he was paying for everything. His money never mattered to me. For him to want to spoil us meant a lot—especially helping my business grow and be more independent.

My cell rang as I pulled up at Kayne's daycare. I helped Kayne out of his car seat and answered the call.

"Hey, Sarai."

"Ew, dryness in your tone! Did I call at a bad time?"

Kayne broke away from my hand when I opened the door to the daycare. "Sorry, how are you?"

"I'm good, calling to give you final information for the party to get you to sign off."

I signed Kayne in, signaled goodbye, and thanked the staff.

"Do you mind meeting at the cakeshop?" Sarai asked.

I threw my purse in the front seat and jumped into the driver's seat, raising my wrist to check the time.

"Sure, I know Laikin has a race today. I planned on being there early."

"Then it works out perfectly. I know Kayne loves chocolate and vanilla. We can meet at Cake Pie in twenty minutes."

"Cake Pie in twenty minutes. Thanks, Sarai."

"No problem. see you soon."

Laikin: You good?
Me: I'm perfect baby.
Laikin: Sarai will call you about the party details.
Me: I just talked to her and meeting her in a few minutes.
Laikin: Keep me updated.
Me: Thank you, Laik.

I would save the talk I had with Virgil for later and not spoil his race today with my drama. As long as Kayne was healthy and safe, that was the only thing that mattered.

*** * ***

Sarai waved her hand in the air, getting my attention in the crowded bakery. I strolled over to the table filled with cake samples and bent down over her, my arms held out for a hug.

"Take a seat. I just got here."

I placed my purse on the back of my chair. "Sorry, a busy day of running errands."

"Please, don't worry. Your man has me running crazy busy. Did he tell you about the magazine interview I scheduled for you both?"

One of the staff members set a glass of water in front of me. "No. What interview?"

"I was able to get you a couples interview and photoshoot together. I thought it would be perfect as an introduction to the world."

"Ugh, I hate being in the spotlight."

Sarai removed a folder from her bag and flipped

through the pages. "I promise it will be tasteful and nothing too crazy."

"Okay."

"So, I wanted to let you know that the party is set and ready to go with a Spiderman theme. I wanted to finalize the cake since we're three weeks out."

"Kayne loves chocolate and vanilla. I try to not give him too many sweets, but it's a special occasion."

"I understand, and I have it planned to be a cake for everybody, and cupcakes on the side."

Sarai dragged her finger from the front of the sheet to the next page, showing the pictures of the cake samples.

"He's going to love that with the Spiderman shaped cake."

"Awesome! He's so cute and I thought having people wear shirts with his face on them would be good."

"Laikin has fought me on paying for everything, but I do think I should contribute something."

The cake chef appeared at the table with a portfolio of her work. "Hello, Sarai. Are you ready to sign off?"

"Padma, this is Amena, Kanye's mother." Sarai introduced us, and I stuck my hand out to shake hers.

"Nice to meet you, Padma."

Padma flipped through the binder on the table. "You as well, Amena. Have you decided on the flavors, or do you need more time?"

I cut into the vanilla and strawberry topping sample, tasting the mixture together. "That is too rich, it would have the kids bouncing off the wall." I washed the flavors down with a glass of water and tasted the chocolate sample. My left brow fluttered at the sweet caramel and chocolate.

Sarai pecked away on her phone.

"The chocolate and caramel, just light on the caramel topping."

Padma scribbled down notes. "Did you want the cupcakes the same?" A soft smile creased her face.

I turned to cast a matching smile. "Have the cupcakes with vanilla only."

Padma walked away with the binder. "I will get on that right away."

Sarai picked up her folder, and I grabbed my bag to follow her out to the cars. "Listen, the cost is taken care of already. Laikin was adamant about covering everything."

I swallowed down my anger. "I hate to be like a taken care of girlfriend. I can handle my own bills."

"When you have a man that loves you and wants to spoil you, let him."

"Malik spoils you?"

Sarai stretched her arm out for a one shoulder hug. "He has no choice, girl. I had his bigheaded child. I better get spoiled."

I laughed and threw a thumbs up and signaled goodbye.

Standing outside my car door, I held it open and yelled, "Send me the magazine details!"

"I got you!" Sarai shouted back.

* * *

A few hours later, I walked through security at the race track, holding Kayne's hand. Winter was right beside me. Security handed us VIP badges, escorting us to the private elevators to get to our section. Laikin always kept his phone on private to focus on work, and I hoped he would take home the big win going into Kayne's birthday.

"Is that little Kayne?" Malik held up his hand for a high-five.

Kayne jumped up to high-five him. "Uncle Malik!"

"What's up, nephew? You got a big birthday coming, right?"

"I do, turning four." Kayne showed four fingers in the air.

The crowd roared as names were called when they pulled out onto the track. Each team came from the pit and waved at the crowd. Laikin smiled and pointed in our direction. I helped Kayne up so he could get a better view.

"Girl, I might find my future husband here," Winter commented, fanning herself. I hugged her shoulder.

All the drivers jumped into their cars, revving their engines. I helped Kayne hold the #1 sign with Laikin's name printed on it.

The event started. Once the warmups finished, the starting light system began sending all the cars into a formation lap. I watched Laikin move in and out at a fast, steady pace. Deep down I worried about his career choices but understood that Formula One racing was his passion.

Laikin's car passed another, which put him in the lead, and set my nerves on the edge as their speeds surpassed hundred miles per hour. Deep down I felt like his biggest cheerleader as I clapped my hands and held up one of the signs Kayne had with his name flashed across it.

"You got this, Laikin!" I jumped in excitement and the crowd became more and more boisterous at him completing each lap. I shielded my eyes from the sun and took a deep breath as the race started come to an end.

"He's going to win. I can feel it." I pressed a hand on Winter's shoulder, and she lifted her hand for a high five.

I scooped Kayne up into my arms to get a better view of the race, when in the blink of an eye, another driver closed in on Laikin and grazed his car hard to the point it pushed him off the ground. I could see he lost control of the wheel from the sound of screeching tires, and the sparks of fire from undercarriage made my stomach drop. The car twisted in circles before it hit the barrier on the side of the track.

My heart beat faster, eyes bulging with the revelation of him being hurt or worse, and anxiety ran high at seeing his car half destroyed on the side of the wall. Winter grasped my hand and we said a silent prayer, as the red flag went up. The rest of the cars slowed down, and we watched medical support speed to him and I scrambled down the bleachers to get a better look. A crew member held a fire extinguisher and sprayed his car. His helmet came off once the scene was safely contained. They moved to pull different straps over him, and I anxiously wanted to run and find out what I could do to help.

"Oh my God! I need to get down there." I handed Kayne over to Winter, and she tugged on my arm.

"Wait! Let them get to him first, Amena. We should go to the hospital."

"He needs me."

"Mommy!" Kayne cried, ran to get in my arms. I took him back to Winter, whispering in his ear.

Bile burned the back of my throat, at the thought of my life without Laikin Trenton. "Shush... everything is okay."

I felt bad not knowing what to tell my son to make him feel better.

"Amena, we have a car to take you to the hospital!" Malik shouted through the crowd.

I walked behind Winter down the bleachers, flanked by security.

"Tell me the truth Malik. Is he all right?"

Malik pushed past the photographer who was trying to get comments. There were flashes of light, and fans screaming my name.

"No comment! Back up." Security pushed people away.

Malik flicked his finger at the valet to open the car doors.

"I will have your car delivered to the hospital," Malik said, horror dawning on his features.

"Honey, I'm going to ride with them." Sarai rolled up beside me.

Winter climbed in first. I got in behind her and passed Kayne over to sit on the opposite side of the three-seater SUV with the tinted windows.

"I got you a police escort," Malik stated, slapping the hood of the car and stepping back directing the crowd.

Sarai typed away on her phone, dialing a number.

I closed my eyes and rubbed my temples. "Please tell me he's going to be all right." My leg wouldn't stop bouncing.

"Laikin is strong. I promise." Sarai patted my thigh.

"Sarai's right, you have to keep praying," Winter said as she started to massage my shoulders.

"Send a statement that we are not commenting on personal health details at this time," Sarai shared over the phone, an edge of fear in her voice. Finally, the car made it to the emergency room. I started to help Kayne out of the car seat, and Winter motioned me away.

"Go, I got him," Winter encouraged, carrying him out of the car behind me.

"Thanks, Winter."

I followed security through the hospital entrance doors. A few people sat together, waiting to be called. Sarai stepped over to the reception desk. I scanned a few of the people's faces. There was exhaustion in their eyes.

"Here to see VIP client, Laikin Trenton," Sarai said.

The moment the words were spoken, everything stopped and became real.

"We have him in a private room. 340 upstairs," the nurse administrator explained.

"Thank you."

My steps felt slow. A knot of tension started to form in my stomach and climbed upward, threatening to choke me. Mentally drained, the closer we got to the elevator the more I worried that life would change forever. Sarai talked with security. Winter kept Kayne preoccupied as I focused on praying for Laikin.

"Remember we're here no matter what, stay calm for Kayne," Winter whispered in my ear. The elevator doors dinged open, and we walked to his door, then gently knocked to enter.

A mischievous grin was pinned to his mouth.

"You're okay." Tears stained my cheeks.

"Pepper, I'm good."

"Laikin!" Kayne wiggled in Winter's arms to get down.

"What's up, lil man." Laikin stiffly moved in the bed, as the nurse checked him out.

"What happened? Is he hurt?"

The nurse scratched something out on the chart and

wrote a new number. "Mr. Trenton is fine—a little sore, but good overall."

Kayne laid on his chest.

I leaned down, kissing him gently on the forehead. "You scared the hell out of me, Laikin."

"Pepper, don't play give me a real kiss." Laikin grunted.

"You need to be careful." I puckered my lips, gazing into his eyes.

"Oh, Mommy! You kissed!" Kayne teased.

"Sorry to worry you, things change so fast, and I lost control for a second." Laikin helped Kayne get off the bed.

"Winter, do you mind taking Kayne home?"

Winter sat up from the couch and grasped Kayne's hand. "Glad you're good, bro." Winter gave him a hug.

"I'm going to stay here tonight."

Laikin captured both of my palms. "Baby, look at me."

I sat on the edge of his bed. "I genuinely thought my life was over."

Laikin reached up to wipe tears from my face. "Never leaving you, sorry to scare you. Love you." His fingers slid over my knuckles.

"I know."

"Malik is in the lobby. I sent a statement to the press already. Glad you're okay, Laikin." Sarai tapped him on shoulder.

"Thanks, Sarai."

"Get some rest—"

Suddenly, the door burst open. We heard a loud, squeaky voice, and security yelling.

"He's my man!" Callie screamed.

"She can't be serious," Sarai spat, marching out of the room.

I jumped up to follow, but Laikin yanked me down.

"Laikin, let me go."

"No, ignore her."

"Ignore her! Are you serious?"

Laikin snaked deeper under the covers. "Callie means nothing to me. She's delusional."

"Oh, I know."

The door opened again to Sarai stomping back over to his bed, arms folded across her chest. "She's banned."

"Thanks again, Sarai."

"I'm glad you figured out this is the woman you need." Sarai pointed at me.

"Believe me, I know who my baby really is." Laikin grinned, then took my mouth in a hot demanding kiss.

"Well, time for me to go. Are you staying?" Sarai asked.

"I am." I pulled back, wiping lipstick from his mouth.

"Baby, go home, I'm good."

"Are you sure?"

"Positive. I'm actually trying to get discharged."

I placed my hand on his forehead like a child to check his temperature. "What? No. You need to stay and get rest."

"Sarai, make sure she gets home and gets some rest."

"Laikin, you need someone here with you."

"Take her with you," Laikin commanded.

I brushed his hand off my lap in a pout.

Sarai and Laikin laughed at me, and I pretended to raise my hand to hit him on the shoulder.

I stayed for a few more hours and talked with Laikin

before heading home, showering, and checking on Kayne in bed. Finally, I thanked Winter for staying with us.

Chapter Fourteen

Laikin

I teased and worked her sweet pussy. The blacker the berry, the sweeter the juice. My tongue circled her clit with a bold swipe. Moisture beaded across my nose and dripped between her legs. Being deep inside her was the safest place in the world for me. A low groan came out when she gripped the top of my head, pushing me deeper into her sweet spot. She was slick and hot. Her hands fisted the sheets, and I needed her body underneath mine. My lust for her was timeless and potent. I pressed and squeezed her thigh over my shoulder.

"Your taste gives me chills."

"I feel the same way." Amena glanced at me, reached for my hand, and tried to bring me to my knees. I traced the lines of her stretch marks on her stomach and thighs, over her beautiful goddess body. Right as I lapped up her nipples, working the firmness in my mouth and sliding my dick in her warmth, we both moaned at the closeness.

"Fuck, this will only be mine."

Her eyes fluttered shut, lights flashed behind my

eyelids as a raging beast of need appeared to make her mine.

Amena brushed a kiss on my cheek, hands moving across my back holding me in a tight embrace.

"Baby, your mouth and pussy have me crazy."

I grunted from the pure animal satisfaction of pleasing her, a savage groan as she squirted from my strokes.

Clasping her hips, she came off the bed meeting me at the brink of climax.

"Let me come...Oh god."

My eruption was near, and I wanted her to be filled with my seed so one day she would have our kids.

Slowly, I slid out of her, tapped my dick two times on her pussy, and rubbed against her lips a few times as she shivered. Amena moaned, her eyes held pure love, and I rammed back inside of her, fucking her to the biggest orgasm of her life.

"Yes! Right there, don't stop."

"I want you to have it all." I pinned her wrists together in my hand.

Amena's pussy squeezed around my dick. I turned around with her on top of me, cupping her ass tight, peppering kisses along her shoulder, while she rolled her hips.

"Baby...." she cooed.

"We have forever."

"Forever." Amena smirked, pulled the covers around our bodies, and snuggled up close.

"Kayne is going to run in here. We have to get up and get dressed, Pepper." I buried my nose in her cheek, ran a hand up and down her leg, and pushed back inside her.

Amena pushed her tongue in my mouth and held on to both sides of my face. "I'm going to miss you."

"Promise to not be gone long."

Amena started to climb off me and I pinched her ass cheek. "Lucky I have a busy day."

"Lucky me. One more and then we'll get up."

Soon as I spoke, a knock on the bedroom door came and Amena moved to get dressed, and answered the door. I slid my boxers on and leaned on the nightstand to check the time, then rushed to wash my hands.

"Mommy, I'm ready." Kayne held onto one of his Spiderman toys.

Amena tightened the robe around her waist and fixed her hair before she let him in the room. "Ready for daycare." Amena lifted Kayne's chin, puckered her lips, and placed a kiss on his cheek. She picked lint off his shirt. She whirled around, winked at me, and swished her hips as she went into the bathroom. Kayne came to the edge of the bed and tried to climb on top. I bent down to pick him up and walked him over to the couch in the corner.

"What are you planning on learning today, Kayne?"

His brows peaked high. "Colors!" Kayne shrieked, kicking his legs up.

I walked into the closet and pulled out a fresh pair of jeans, shirt, and jacket, then laid them on top of the bed to prepare for the shower in another room.

"Are you hungry?"

Kayne raised his toy in the air, pretending to fly. "Yep."

"Let's give Mommy some time to shower and dress." I took him by the hand and walked to the kitchen. I reached down, picked him up, and put him on top of the island of my condo.

"Bacon and eggs coming right up."

Today wasn't too crazy, and I planned on asking Amena to move in with me here. If she wanted to keep her condo, I had no problem with helping her lease it out. I flipped the bacon in the skillet, cut more apples and bananas, and poured orange juice.

"Start eating and stay here. I have to go shower." I raised my hand and felt the top of his curls. Amena came in the kitchen and pecked me on the cheek. I tossed my dirty laundry in the bin, squeezed minty toothpaste on the brush, and started to clean up. An hour later I pushed the solid oak door closed, helped Kayne in his car seat, and pressed the garage gate to open as Amena turned down the radio.

"What's your day looking like?" I scanned the mirror to check on Kayne in the back seat.

The cool weather breezed through the open windows. Amena laid her hand on top of mine. "I have a few meetings, but nothing major."

We arrived at a small bakery a few minutes from Kayne's daycare to pick up what she'd ordered yesterday, since it was his week to bring donuts for everyone. I handed Kayne a glazed donut, removed my wallet, and paid with a twenty-dollar bill.

After Kayne was dropped off, Amena got a call about work. While holding the door open, I assisted Amena sliding in the car, putting her seatbelt on, and watched her end the call.

"What do you think about moving in with me?"

"Seriously?"

"We're committed to each other, right?"

Amena leaned across the seat, wrapping her arms around my neck in a tight hug.

I put the car in park in front of her building downtown, a slew of photographers stood around, and I blew out a breath of annoyance.

"Are you sure about moving in together?"

"More than you know." I shut the door behind her, grasped her by the left hand, and escorted her through the crowd. A few photographers yelled out rude comments, which we ignored.

"Laikin! Can we get a picture?" Amena joked. I slapped her on the ass.

"Get done what you need to do and later we can do dinner."

Amena stood on her tippy toes, wrapping her arms around my waist. "Give me a kiss."

"What if we take a vacation?"

Tenderness glowed in her eyes. "Where? Don't you race soon?"

"I do, but we can take a quick trip, Kayne, Brett, and our parents."

"A family trip."

I gazed fiercely at her, ready to take her . "A family trip."

Amena's phone rang, and she checked the name before answering. "I need to take this call, call me later."

I picked up her hand, pressed a kiss to it, then left so she could get her work done.

* * *

The bar was crowded, and I raised my head at the guard, who allowed me to enter. A few faces sparkled when I strolled by and walked up next to Brett and Kash.

Brett held a hand up for a dap and shake. The bartender walked to the edge and placed a menu in front of me.

"A bottle of water is fine."

He gave me a sideways glance. "What's so important you had us meet you here?" Brett chugged the bottle.

"I asked Amena to move in with me."

Kash and Brett choked on their drink.

"That's fast."

"To you, but we have years between us."

Kash's smile tugged at his lips. "Amena's good for you."

"Thanks, Kash."

"As long as my sister is happy, I have no complaints."

"Cool because I already got the movers going to her condo to get things started." A mischievous grin pinned to my mouth.

His eyebrows furrowed as he frowned. "Any news from Callie lately?"

"After Sarai put out the last statement, we haven't heard a word." One thing I could give Sarai was a thank-you for getting me out of the playboy mindset and more into the business mindset. I slowed down on a lot of stuff and after winning a few months back, I wanted to be even more focused on my goals.

"Amena is working more, and before I get busy, I want to take her on a trip with the family."

"Where are you planning on going?"

"Belize."

"She'll love it."

"I agree, and I want you guys to come with us—and your families."

"I will check with Arianna, but you know she loves driving," Kash replied.

"I'm down." Brett forced his chin upwards.

Amena deserved the world, and she deserved me to spoil her. Kayne was priority number one. I lifted my vibrating phone to see her sending me a heart emoji.

"Fill me in on the details and I can see what my schedule looks like at work."

"Gotcha, bro."

Brett, Kash, and I laughed and joked, while the TV played coverage of the basketball playoffs.

Later, I picked up my ringing phone as I jumped in my car to leave.

"Sarai, am I your favorite?"

"Favorite asshole client."

I chuckled as I started the car. "What's up?"

"I got your text about a trip you're taking."

Sarai knew me better than anyone and hated it when I added things to her plate last minute. "We're going on a trip with our families."

"When is the trip happening?"

"In a month if possible."

"Laikin, you have major deals coming on board."

"They can be rescheduled for afterwards."

Sarai groaned. "I hate you."

"Why don't you and Malik come with us?"

"No, I have too much to do. Let me move some stuff around."

"Thanks, Sarai."

"All about you, Laikin," Sarai teased, hanging up the call.

My parents were both home so I shut the car off, placed my phone in my pocket, and unlocked the front door. Pops sat at the dining table, reading the paper.

I clapped him on the shoulder. "Old man, what's shaking?"

He placed the newspaper down on the table and removed his glasses. "Sitting and enjoying my day with my woman." The gray hairs in his beard gave me a glimpse of how I would look at his age.

"Where's Ma?"

"In the basement, doing laundry."

I walked to the kitchen, opened the fridge, grabbed a bottle of water, then sat down next to him.

"I asked Amena to move in with me."

"A big step for you."

"It's time, we're not kids anymore."

"Being a parent is tough. You ready for that responsibility?"

"Kayne makes it easy."

The basement door opened. Mom smiled, holding a basket of clothes. "Hey, sweetie pie." Mom dropped the basket on the floor next to the table.

"Ma, you good?"

"Great. Sweetie. How are Amena and Kayne?"

Dad cupped the coffee in his hand. "He's moving her into his house."

"A ring must be coming if you're moving in together." Mom grinned, rubbed her hands together.

I sat straight up. "In the future."

"Amena has to think about her son. I expect you to not string her along." Mom wagged a finger in my face.

"Damn, am I that bad?" I folded my arms.

Mom strode next to me and patted me on the shoulder. "My love for you will never stop, but I am a woman first, and I know how men can sell you dreams."

"All right, Ma, I got you. Amena's not going anywhere because I love her."

"Then we support you, sweetie. Are you hungry?"

I tapped my watch to check the time. "I need to get going so I can make sure the movers have finished moving Amena's stuff."

"Call us if you need us," Mom said, arm extended forward for a hug.

* * *

Driving from the condo to pick up Amena and Kayne, then heading home, felt like the best day and gave me a sense of balance. Kayne jumped around in excitement at winning the basketball game, while his mom was in the kitchen cooking dinner. The movers had the bigger items moved over and their clothes. I told Amena we could get the rest tomorrow before I go back to work.

"Kayne, what do you want for you birthday?"

"A party!"

"Let me guess—a Spiderman party?" We had made sure that his room was decorated in Spiderman stuff.

Amena put her wine glass to her lips. I stood at the side, watching Amena sway her hips to the music, while pouring wine in the other pan on top of the stove. She turned oven down with her baked chicken.

"Try this and tell me if you like it with the sauce." Amena's lips pulled together to blow over the heat.

The spiciness filled my tongue. "Good one, baby."

Amena wiped her hands on the towel and pulled out plates and cups for dinner. "Can you set the table?"

"I talked to Sarai about clearing my schedule."

Amena turned to me. "She give you shit?"

"A little, but she understood."

"I'm excited to go on our first trip as a family."

"First, but not the last."

"Kayne, turn the TV off and come eat." Amena pulled the chicken out, filling a plate for him and placing it on the table.

Kayne ran into the kitchen and took a seat.

"Sarai scheduled the interview."

Amena gulped her drink. "I'm excited, but nervous."

"Me too."

Kayne ate a piece of cornbread, sitting up in his chair. "Hungry!" Kayne laughed with his mouth open.

* * *

After Amena gave him a bath, I sat on the other side of the bed as she read him a bedtime story.

"The tiger went home." Amena pretended to growl like an animal.

Kayne laughed at her attempt. She leaned forward and pressed a kiss on his cheek, then his forehead.

"Laikin, can you stay until I go to sleep?" Kayne asked as I stood to leave.

I looked from him to Amena.

"Are you scared of the dark baby?" Amena had a night light in the corner for him and kept the door open in case he wanted to come sleep with us.

"No, Mommy, this is *man* talk," Kayne answered, making both of us gawk at his statement.

"Ugh, okay. I will leave you two alone." Her shoulders dropped like she was missing out on something.

I shrugged and sat back on the bed. "What's going on, little man?"

"Do you love my mommy?"

"I do."

"Does that mean you like me?"

I smiled at his question. "I like you a lot."

"Can you be my daddy?"

I hadn't thought to even talk with Amena about my role in her son's life and now, having this conversation, it felt like we should have talked with him sooner about my intentions.

"You know your dad's name is Virgil right?"

He nodded, twisting his teddy bear in his hands. "He no fun like you."

"Thanks, little man. I tell you what."

"What?"

"I promise to always be here for you and have fun, and you never have to question if I'm in your corner."

"Okay."

"Get some sleep."

A family dinner, tucking a kid into bed, and falling in bed with the love of my life like this? I hoped it would last for more years to come, with additional kids laughing and playing together. Amena had brought more to my life than I could ever imagine.

Chapter Fifteen

Amena

Three Weeks Later

I got out of the limo holding Laikin's hand. Sarai directed us to the dressing room. I smiled at the team that would be assisting today.

"Amena, you're in this room. Laikin, you're next door," Sarai said.

"Thanks, Sarai."

"Why can't we share?" Laikin suggested.

I stuck my tongue out jokingly. "Because we need you to be ready on time."

The makeup and hairstylist laughed. Sarai threw her head back in laughter, too.

Sarai shoved Laikin to the side. "Exactly. Amena, you understand the stress he brings me."

I climbed in the makeup chair, placed my purse on the top of the vanity table, unwrapped my shawl, and removed my shades.

"How long are we scheduled?"

"No more than seven hours. They know we have a party tomorrow," Sarai responded.

"Okay."

"Relax, get pretty, and have fun."

Sarai walked away. I used a makeup wipe on my face. The hairstylist pulled my hair out of my ponytail and combed through my wet strands. One of the assistants held up the clothes that I would model for the shoot.

"The theme is casual and classy."

"I like the cream sweater dress with the boots." I swiveled my head around and pointed to the pieces.

"For the set that would work and then we'll move to you standing near the car," the assistant said.

"The black leather pants and silk blouse is cute."

"Awesome, we have few minutes to make any changes, then you get two hours to get ready." The hairstylist brushed over my hair. "It won't take long."

"I have my son's birthday party tomorrow."

"I have two kids myself," Rachel, the hairstylist explained.

"I have one so I can only imagine two." I sighed through a long-held breath.

"Being a mom is hard work—especially when you're single," Rachel preached, and I agreed with a nod. Laikin told me about the conversation with Kayne.

I came out of the dressing room wearing the sweater dress, with my hair pulled into a tight bun, diamonds in my ears, and a watch on my wrist. Laikin talked with Sarai on set. A mix of old-school hip hop played, starting with Biz Markie.

"You both look great, so we'll do a few shots and then

start the interview," said the reporter from Men Style magazine I met earlier.

"Stand right here?" I wondered, putting my hand on my hip.

"Sit in his lap on the couch, and then we'll do a few poses separately." The photographer snapped a few shots as the lighting was moved closer.

"Okay."

Laikin extended his arm around my waist, whispering, "I'm ready to rip this dress off you."

I glanced up at him. "Behave."

He winked at me. "Shit, you looking too good."

I reached to cup his chin. "You look handsome, Mr. Trenton."

"Keep that pose!" the photographer yelled, coming in closer in front of us.

I crossed my legs, clasped my hands together, and looked to the side of his face as he stared forward in the camera.

"Right, keep that pose—both of you."

Laikin ran a hand up and down my thigh, and I remembered our early morning connection and his head between my thighs.

"Promise to wear this cologne again."

Laikin peered at me. "Making my dick hard, Pepper."

I smirked. "Pay attention before Sarai yells at us."

"Sarai knows you can get it anytime."

"Anytime?"

"Anytime, baby."

"All right, one more with Amena standing up—and Laikin, hold her around the waist," Sarai demanded.

I jumped up and held a hand to my side, looking up

into the camera. "Yes! Hold that pose," the photographer said.

I truly felt accepted and loved by Laikin and his family. Kayne even wanted to call him Dad. I tried to explain the difference, but if he felt comfortable and loved by Laikin, then I wouldn't deny him—especially after Virgil sent the paperwork to give up his parental rights two weeks ago.

"Okay, let's take some questions, and then change outfits." The staff brought out a chair for the reporter to take a seat, and I sat beside Laikin, holding his hand.

"Thank you both for being here today. I know a lot of your fans have heard the story of you two being in love at a young age," Jalesa brought up, turning on the recorder.

Laikin stared at me. "She broke my heart," he joked, and I rolled my eyes.

"He's so dramatic."

"We'll delve deeper into the background later, but for now how does it feel dating a super star athlete like Laikin?" Jalesa sat back in her chair.

"At first, it was chaos, honestly. I know Sarai probably hates me for using that word, but I had to adjust. Not only in the relationship, I also have a child."

"Which is commendable. A lot of people can relate to being a single mom. You were married correct? To a high-profile politician?" Jalesa flipped through her notes.

"I was, and I promised myself to never date anyone that was known in the media again, but coming home and seeing him changed my mind."

"I gave her a hard time in the beginning, but Amena is meant for me," Laikin replied.

"Did you ever feel like you two wouldn't make it, Laikin?"

Laikin rubbed his hands together. "At first, I denied my feelings, but seeing how she had changed over the years and talking about our past made me want to try again."

"Amena, you're a celebrity stylist. Does it conflict with being Laikin's girlfriend at all?"

"Actually, in the beginning, I refused his help and complained about going out with him. I tried to keep my son away from the media, and nothing worked, because I was too stubborn to let go of the past."

"As women we do carry a lot of the burden," Jalesa reminded me.

"Yeah, we do. Laikin is genuine and amazing. He helped jumpstart my career and believed in me when I had doubts."

"She's the best."

"We're still seeing posts about Callie mentioning your man. How do you respond?"

"Callie who?"

Laikin and Jalesa laughed at my response.

"Well, I guess that means we should move on," Jalesa said.

"Only thing we're concerned about is our family, nothing else can stop our relationship."

"What do you have planned for the future? I know Laikin is racing again after the last scare."

"He acts like it was nothing, but it was big deal. For me I'll be taking more time to really flourish in my business while also being a productive mom to my son."

"My love of racing continues, and I know the last race scared her a little, but it's all good now. Being around Amena and seeing how hard she works makes me want to work even harder," Laikin stated.

"I love a power couple. Thank you both for being here today."

"Thank you," we answered at the same time.

Jalesa wrapped up her interview, and we rose from the couch as the set was starting to clear out.

"Okay, you two go change, please. My godson has not stopped texting me about his party." Sarai turned her phone around to show us a text thread from Kayne.

Kaynebear: Auntie, when?
Sarai: Baby tomorrow
Kaynebear: I ready now.

I chuckled at the frown emoji attached to his text.

"That boy is spoiled. I know Malik pissed me off getting him a Freddo Mercedes Benz truck." I wanted to curse him out when I saw the gold rims on the toy car in our yard.

"That's his friend." Sarai directed her finger at Laikin.

The rest of the afternoon was filled with laughter, jokes, and music while we finished off the shoot doing single poses and then couple shots. Laikin took a few pictures with the staff and gave autographs before we left and drove home.

* * *

The doorbell rang, and the last guests arrived as I helped my mom set out the rest of the gift bags. Sarai did so much and made Kayne's birthday an event with professional photographers stationed to take pictures, a photo booth, pony ride section, and an actual valet to park the cars. When Laikin told me the final cost, I really had no words for how much I appreciated her work to make sure every detail was checked off the list. Winter held a cocktail in her hand, swaying her hips to the DJ playing Arianna Grande. Kayne hadn't sat down for five minutes and talked our heads off about his birthday being an official day every day.

"That boy is never going to sleep tonight." Winter grinned at Kayne, who was wearing his Spiderman outfit. All the kids dressed in superhero costumes.

"He's having a ball."

"You did good, Amena."

"Thank you. His joy is worth all the headaches."

"I agree. Have you looked at the comments on his live."

"What live?"

"Laikin got on live when you were in the bathroom a few minutes ago and showed off the party."

"He never shows his place."

"Which tells you how important you and Kayne are to him. Let me see if I can catch a screen grab of the comments." Winter slipped her phone from her shorts.

"Kayne, slow down before you fall," I grumbled, catching him by the arm as he ran in the direction of the food table. A comforting breeze and sunshine made today perfect for a party. Laikin couldn't go to Disneyland, so Sarai transformed his backyard into the ultimate kids' fantasy, with large balloons of every superhero, from Wolverine to Captain America. An entertainment booth on one end for DJ, a face painting table across from a bouncy house, and a sweets stand on the other.

"Sorry, Mommy." Kayne ran into my legs, hugging me.

I tapped him on the back. "Be careful."

Winter handed me her phone. "Here's the comments."

"Wow, it has close to ten thousand comments on here."

"You should go live really quick and respond."

I handed the phone back. "I hate social media."

"Just this once." Winter turned on her live and held the phone up in my face. I waved to the camera with a wide smile.

"What's up, everybody? I'm here with my girl, Amena. Say hi."

"Winter, really."

She popped her lips. "Yep. What do you think about the party?"

"Glad to see my baby happy."

"That's right and your man is making sure of that, right? Mr. Laikin Trenton?"

"He is the best, but never let the smile fool you. He belongs to me."

A chain of people were online, commenting hi, and how much they loved Laikin and me, and how we were couple goals. Then the live turned even busier when Laikin popped in from across the backyard.

Laikin's top lip curled up. "Who you belong to, Amena?"

"I belong to Laikin Trenton."

"Exactly, never doubt it. Make sure they know, because I hate to get on here and act a fool on somebody."

"Daddy!" Kayne screamed, running toward Laikin.

"Kayne, be careful."

"My girl is the top stylist. Make sure you hit her up," Laikin boasted.

"Thank you, baby."

A few hearts popped up on the thread, and some not-so-nice comments, but I ignored them and focused on the positive ones.

"All right, folks, we have a birthday party to get to. Make sure you follow us."

"We should bring the cake out," my mom said as she came up to me. Rebuilding our relationship had taken time, and distance helped. They're way better grandparents with Kayne, spoiling him nonstop.

"Okay, he's going to want to get in the pool soon."

Dad grabbed him up, tickling his stomach. Laikin approached me, tugging me in his arms. "You having fun?"

I peered up at him. "I am, we're going to bring the cake out."

"Soon as the part is over, we need to have a private party."

"Private party, huh?"

I turned in his arms, extended my arms around his neck, and pecked him on the lips. Laikin smacked me on the ass.

"This is a kids' party. Watch your hands, bro." Brett held a frown, making Laikin shrug while keeping his hands on my butt.

"Brett, what hussy did you bring to my baby's party?"

"She's cool peoples. Her name is Noelle."

Noelle stood in line to get a drink form the bar in the corner.

I drifted in front of Laikin, arms folded. "It serious?"

"We're dating."

"What about Winter?"

"Winter is minding her business." Winter came over

holding her drink. Brett tried to take her drink out her hands, but she smacked it down.

"You two act like kids in love," I joked.

"Only we won't end up like you and Laikin," Brett teased, and I stuck out my tongue at him.

Laikin chuckled along with Winter, as my mom came out with the cake. Sarai, Malik, and all the other parents joined in, making us move in closer, as Kayne ran out of the bouncy house.

"Happy Birthday to you, Kayne."

Kayne blew out the candles. "Thank you, Mommy and Laikin."

"You are so welcome."

* * *

Winter, Brett, and Kayne posed in front of the camera with our parents with the bright sun behind them on the beach. I watched him enjoy himself when Laikin held him around his neck. Our trip was beyond peaceful and relaxing. A two-week trip eating, having sex, and ignoring work was exactly what we needed. Laikin let Kayne down and jogged over to wrap his arms around my waist.

"What are you doing over here?" Laikin pecked me on the lips.

"Watching my man."

"My baby enjoying herself?"

"Yes, I am, and ready for another night of you fucking me good."

"Shush, I might have to kick your brother's ass. He wants to go to some club."

"Brett needs to focus on his love life and leave you

alone." I watched Brett pick Winter up over his shoulder and run into the ocean, and she pounded on his back.

"Mommy!"

"Kayne." I watched as he built a sandcastle.

"Come on, let's go help our son."

Epilogue

Laikin

Two years passed, and my career went to even greater heights than I imagined after I won the Daytona 500. I became a married father of twins, and adopted Kayne, who was now six years old, and the best big brother. No matter what, the babies went to him for everything, and Amena sometimes had to fight for their attention, because they were always running behind him. Like right now we were on our way to the *Essence* Women in Hollywood awards for Amena. After her work with Marlowe made a splash in high profile magazines caused her to get picked up worldwide, we flew around to different countries for fashion shows.

After the birth of the twins, I took time off from racing and focused on my family, taking Kayne to school and traveling with Amena, while she worked and breastfed the kids. I kind of turned into Mr. Mom, but I loved my role. We also swapped every few months to support each other's work. I focused more on youth-center fundraising to give children more access to after-school programs. Once the *Essence* banquet is over, we have our two-year anniversary party at Kash and Arianna's house. As soon as the limo arrived at the venue, both boys got rowdy, trying to get out of their car seats. LJ and Kodey mimicked everything that Kayne did.

"I love you," she said, her voice sounding breathy as she pulled back from giving me a peck on the lips. My driver opened the door and helped her out first, and she waved at the fans and reporters. Kayne climbed out next, then LJ stretched his arms out for his brother, and I watched to make sure that he wouldn't fall. Coming out on the other side of the limo, I picked up Kodey, checking to make sure that he didn't mess up his tux from his bottle. Amena grasped both boys' hands and posed for pictures, while I stood off to the side, as reporters called her name.

"Amena over here! What's your boy's name?" a reporter screamed.

I shook my head at the constant barrage of reporters trying to find out any personal information. We normally kept the kids out of the spotlight—especially on social media. When Sarai got an offer of a million dollars for us to do an interview and take pictures for a magazine, we declined because our kids never asked for this life. Kayne was already known because of how I acted in the beginning, but that made us take a step back and become more private.

Amena's long, pink, silk-and-lace backless gown draped on the floor. Marlowe surprised her and came up to hug and pose with her.

"Amena did you style Marlowe for today?" Another reporter jumped in to get answers.

"I wouldn't walk out the house without Amena's

touch." Marlowe puffed her lips together and blew a kiss to the cameras.

Amena turned her head toward me and extended her hand for me to come closer. I crammed in beside her, still holding Kodey in my left arm.

"I don't think I can ever get used to you being my wife."

Amena eyes raised up to gaze into mine. "All yours and more."

"Laikin, Amena, are you ready to go inside?" Sarai appeared and reached for Kodey. I handed him over. Kayne held onto LJ's hand.

"Lead the way, boss." I planted a hand on Amena's lower back.

Essence had a pink-and-cream theme, with roses in every corner, and pictures of each nominee hung on the walls. People packed the room and our parents decided to stay back to make sure everything was ready for the party. Malik came up, shook hands with me, and kissed Amena on the cheek.

"Watch those lips, bro," I chastised, pretending to shadow box with my hands.

Malik held both hands up in surrender. "We know that's your wife, bro. No need to fight over that big fat ring that's blinding people even a mile away," Malik jested, holding up Amena's hand.

"Have to let all these busters know what's up." I linked our hands together.

"Baby, the boys," Amena whispered, pointing at them.

"Your table's right up front. Marlowe's presenting the award to you." Sarai headed in the direction of our table.

Right as we made it to the table, the boys took a seat.

Sarai talked with the waitstaff to get drinks for everyone. A few celebrities approached Amena to meet her. I stayed to the side in admiration.

"Thanks, we can for sure set something up." Amena finished her conversation and sat next to me. I took her by the hand and squeezed, as the announcer of *Essence* magazine came up to the podium.

"Before we begin, I want to thank everyone for coming out today, and to start off correctly, we're presenting the first honor to Amena Trenton, the stylist of the year and soon to be Fashion editor of *Essence* magazine." The Vice President of the magazine winked at Amena. Caught by the surprise announcement, I cupped her chin, captured her lips, and sucked on her bottom lip, ready to take her back home and show her how much she was appreciated.

"Keep that up we'll never get to our party." Amena wiped the lipstick off my lips, rising out of the chair, and kissed each boy on the top of his head. I removed my phone from my pocket to take pictures and video. Marlowe held up the award and spoke. Kayne started to get up and run to the stage, and Kodey tried to follow, but I stopped him from climbing off his seat.

"Amena, I tell you all the time what a great eye for detail you have, knowing the perfect fit for people's personalities." Marlowe pushed the microphone closer.

The entire room cheered and roared in excitement, then Marlowe stepped to the side and let Amena speak.

"Thank you, Marlowe, the entire fashion industry, and the magazines that have supported my journey. Most of all, I want to thank my family and friends for sticking by me—especially the love of my life, Mr. Laikin Trenton." Amena pointed at our table.

I blew a kiss to her and picked up Kodey to sit on my lap. As soon as she finished, we continued to talk and celebrate, before leaving to get to our anniversary party.

* * *

Loud music and claps echoed throughout the living room as the boys ran through the front door. I took Amena by the arm and helped her remove her shawl, greeting our family and friends. Brett slapped hands with me, giving a man hug, and I reached my parents with a hug and kiss. Pictures of our kids and our wedding were hung around the room. We walked out to the backyard, with more friends and extended family coming up to us. I held Amena's right hand, then pointed to the table full of gifts.

"Two years of marriage, and three kids." Kash passed a drink to me.

"Taking after you, bro."

I let go of Amena's hand so she could greet our friends. Malik and Sarai arrived from the event a few minutes after us.

"When did we become our parents?" Brett shook his head, gulping the drink down.

I scanned the backyard and then I noticed all my friends were married with kids now, no longer the playboy bachelors.

Amena interlocked our arms, laid her head on my shoulder, and I kissed the top of her head.

The music roared around us. "Proud of you."

"Proud of us," Amena replied, as our three boys ran around the yard engulfed with their friends and cousins.

The day Amena and I reconnected, letting the hate go had never been more freeing than when she accepted my proposal on that same road when we took a drive up the coast.

Remembering my plan, we pulled to the side of the road, and I pretended to check something from the engine, then got her out of the car and dropped to my knee.

"Laikin, are you serious?" Amena held a hand over her mouth in shock.

I captured her hand, kissed her palm, and held the two-carat ring in my hand.

"Amena, will you do me the honor and be my wife?"

Cars drove by and honked. Tears poured down Amena's cheeks as she nodded her head.

"I need words, Pepper."

"Yes, I will marry you." Amena threw her hands around my neck, smashing our lips together.

Snapping her fingers in my face, she said, "Laikin." Her lips were pressed shut in confusion.

"Come here." I bent my head down, capturing her lips.

The softness of her pouty lips and our tongues clashing together caused me to back up and put a little space between us before we ended up making another baby.

Amena brushed her hand across my lips, cleaning up the excess lipstick. "What are you dreaming about?"

"Life with you."

"Daddy, can we play the car game?" Kayne ran up with his brothers trailed behind.

Amena reached down to pick up Kodey. "Kayne, I don't want you to get dirty."

My boys loved pretending to be race car drivers, and pretending to work on cars so I got custom uniforms like mine with their names on the back. We'd go to the K1 and race for fun. I even wanted to have a track built in the backyard, but Amena shot that down.

"You ready to ride, Kayne?" I placed a hand on top of his head, ruffling his curls.

"Yes! Come on, Mom, can I please go?"

"Just like your father."

I buried my head in her neck, whispering in her ear. "You can ride *me* later."

Amena's eyes fluttered, lust taking control.

"Let's go, son." I fished my keys out of my pocket, taking Kayne by the hand and leading us out.

Check Out More from Chiquita Dennie

I hope you enjoyed **Amena** and **Laikin's story.** If you want to see more of these characters, then check out bonus scenes here: https://chiquitadennie.squarespace.com/bonus-scenes, and start the series from the beginning with Kash and Arianna.
Ethan and Maya has a story to tell in **Bossy Billionaire** here: https://bit.ly/3uB50BC
Follow the TN Seal Security series with the standalone, opposites-attract, fake-dating, military romance **Nicco** here: https://bit.ly/47ZZN6p
Are you a fan of sports romance? Then download the one-night stand, billionaire romance **Refuel** here: https://bit.ly/3RqFx8l
Also, follow it up with the workplace, sports romance **Pressure** here: https://bit.ly/3RqagT1
If you love romantic comedy, fake relationships, and enemies-to-lovers, then find it in **Something Gained** here: https://bit.ly/3OwGbiP.
My stories of friends finding love started with the Heart

of Stone series, which includes a host of characters and families. It starts with **Broken** (Emery and Jackson, Book 1), a sports, one-night-stand, workplace romance found here: https://bit.ly/3hxVavF

Then you can continue with a fun side-story about Emery and Jackson with their **Valentine's Day Short** here: https://bit.ly/42ttg7o

Emery's best friend Jordan's story continues in **Rebirth** (Book 2), a single-dad, widow, billionaire romance: https://bit.ly/3YiQtGS

Hop on and download **Reveal** with Angela and Brent here: https://bit.ly/3OupYur

If you love bonus content, then click here for bonus scenes: https://chiquitadennie.squarespace.com/bonus-scenes

Please also check out a second-chance, workplace romance with a host of characters intertwined in **Renew** (Book 4) here: https://bit.ly/3w0rgHi

Follow Desiree and Gabriel in **Temptation**, a standalone, contemporary, sports, curvy girl romance here: https://bit.ly/42r8ODQ

Check out the dark mafia romance that started my journey with Antonio and Sabrina in **Ruthless** (Book 1) here: https://bit.ly/3iS64XT

Antonio and Sabrina's relationship continues in **Savage** (Book 2), as they get to know each other and their families here: https://bit.ly/3w77CJT

Antonio and Sabrina have more work to do in **Beast** (Book 3) here: https://bit.ly/3Untivm

Did you know that **Janice and Carlo** have a book? Well, grab this dark mafia romance with emotional scars and betrayal here: https://bit.ly/42yJBaH

Any fans of forbidden political romance? Check out the steamy romance **Mutual Agreement** here: https://bit.ly/3OyAzod

Do you love workplace romantic suspense? Then check out **Aydin** here: https://bit.ly/496jKcv

Also, check out the interconnected standalone, hate-to-love, damsel-in-distress, actress-and-bodyguard romance **Nasir** here: https://bit.ly/3uovwQr

Have you checked out **She's All I Need**, a sports, opposites-attract romance? Click here: https://books2read.com/u/49lkeW

How about a dark romance that has everything, from steamy romance to opposites-attract, suspense, thriller, celebrities, and more? Read **Stolen** (Book 1) here: https://books2read.com/u/mvZlgV

Don't miss Joaquin and Sofia's follow-up story in **Saved** (Book 2) here: https://books2read.com/u/4DWwLd

The conclusion for Joaquin and Sofia comes full circle in **Betrayed** (Book 3) here: https://books2read.com/u/4A5LGp

Catch up with your favorite characters in the holiday short romance (includes spoilers) **Holiday Collection** here: https://books2read.com/u/bzd59G

For small-town, single-mom stories, check out **Until Seren**a here: https://books2read.com/u/mej8vr

Do you love fun billionaire romances? If so, then check out **Cocky Catcher**, a sports, enemies-to-lovers romance, here: https://bit.ly/3R57VeT

Are you a reader of sports workplace romance? Then grab **Scoring with Sadie**, a workplace, enemies-to-lovers romance, here: https://bit.ly/3nkWhBp

All curvy girl, plus-size romance lovers should get into **I**

Deserve His Love, a standalone, second-chance romance here: https://books2read.com/u/mVrGwP Finally, fantasy romance readers should look no further than **Red Light District**, a curvy girl, fling romance: https://books2read.com/u/m2RQ6G

Struck of Love Universe

The Early Years-A Prequel
https://books2read.com/u/49Zjnw
Ruthless Struck In Love Book 1
https://books2read.com/u/4AxKLo
Savage Struck In Love Book 2
https://books2read.com/u/bpED6g
Beast Struck In Love Book 3
https://books2read.com/u/3LpgdJ
Janice and Carlo Captivated By His Love
https://books2read.com/u/b6je6M
Brutal Struck In Love Book 4
https://books2read.com/u/4NQyE9
Stolen-Fuertes Mafia Cartel Book 1
https://books2read.com/u/mvZlgV
Saved-Fuertes Mafia Cartel Book 2
https://books2read.com/u/4DWwLd
Redemption Struck In Love Book 5
https://books2read.com/u/b5kZ8O
Betrayal- Fuertes Mafia Cartel Book 3
https://books2read.com/u/4A5LGp

Heart of Stone Universe

Broken 1 Emery and Jackson
https://books2read.com/u/boWPAV
Heart of Stone Book 1.5
https://payhip.com/b/kWg7
Rebirth 2 Jordan and Damon
https://books2read.com/u/ba2OMx
Heart of Stone Book 3.5 Bottoms Up
https://payhip.com/b/HGP1
Reveal 3 Angela and Brent
https://books2read.com/u/31rx9l
Renew 4 Jessica and Joseph
https://books2read.com/u/4NXyPG

Also By Chiquita Dennie

Series

<u>Struck in Love</u>

The Early Years-A Prequel Short Story

Ruthless:Antonio and Sabrina Book 1

Savage: Antonio and Sabrina Book 2

Beastl: Antonio and Sabrina Book 3

Captivated By His Love:Janice and Carlo

Brutal: Antonio and Sabrina Booke 4

Redemption: Antonio and Sabrina Book 5

<u>Heart of Stone</u>

Broken, Book 1 (Emery & Jackson)

A Valentine's Day Short Book 1.5 Emery & Jackson

Rebirth, Book 2 (Jordan and Damon)

Reveal, Book 3 (Angela and Brent)

Bottoms Up Book 3.5 Jessica and Joseph Short

Renew, Book 4 (Jessica and Joseph)

<u>Cocky Billionaire Boys</u>

Cocky Catcher (Cocky Billionaire Boys Book 1)

Bossy Billionaire (Cocky Billionaire Boys Book 2)

The Fuertes Cartel

Stolen (The Fuertes Cartel Book 1)
Saved (The Fuertes Cartel Book 2)
Betrayed (The Fuertes Cartel Book 3)

Carrington Cartel

Torn: The Carrington Cartel Book 1
Claim: The Carrington Cartel Book 2

Something

Something Gained: A Romantic Comedy Book 1
Something Earned: A Romantic Comedy Book 2

Pierce Motors

Refuel:(Pierce Motors Book l)
Pressure:(Pierce Motors Book 2)

Summer Break

Summer Nights(Summer Break Book 1)

TN Seal Security

Aydin: Book 1
Nasir: Book 2
Nicco: Book 3

Standalones

Until Serena(HEA World Novel)
Temptation
She's All I Need
I Deserve His Love
Mutual Agreement

Scoring with Sadie
Exposed (A Bodyguard Novel)
Love Shorts:A Collection of Short Stories
Red Light District(A Fantasy Romance Short)

<u>By Keke Renée:</u>
Wet Heat
His Peace, Her Pleasure
Baby, It's Cold Outside
Love Don't Live Here Anymore, Book 1, 2
Every Time We Touch (A Wet Heat Novelette)
One Night Only- Love By Design Book 1
Cassian and Savannah Love By Design Book 2
Deidra's Love -Love By Design Book 3
Protecting Bria: Book 1
Protecting Chanel:Book 2
Protecting Yanira: Book 3
Haven: A Single Dad Romance
Sensual
Seek to Please: Book 1
Seek To Touch: Book 2
Seek To Bare:Book 3
Seek To Love: Book 4
Seek To Trust: Book 5
Seek To Earn: Book 6
Tease Me: Book 1
Promise Me: Book 1

<u>By Ava S.King</u>
Fatal Memory: Book 1 Teagan Stone
Fatal Target: Book 2 Teagan Stone
Fatal Crime: Book 3 Teagan Stone
Fatal Justice: Book 4 Teagan Stone

Fatal Enemy: Book 5 Teagan Stone
Fatal Death: Book 6 Teagan Stone
Fatal Revenge: Book 7 Teagan Stone
Fatal Pursuit: Book 8 Teagan Stone
Mirror of Lies: Book 1
Mirror of Lust: Book 2
Ruined: Andi Easton Book 1
Thank you so much for reading and if you enjoyed the crazy ride and decide to leave a review we'd truly appreciate the support..

About the Author

Chiquita Dennie is an author of Contemporary, Romantic Suspense, Erotic, and Women's Fiction.

Chiquita lives in Los Angeles, CA. Before she started writing contemporary romance, she worked in the entertainment industry on notable TV shows such as the Dr. Phil show, the Tyra Banks show, American Idol, and Deal or No Deal. But her favorite job is the one she's now doing: full-time writing romance.

A best-selling author and award-winning filmmaker, her first short film, "Invisible," was released in summer 2017 and screened in multiple festivals and won for Best Short Film. She also hosts a podcast that showcases the latest in beauty, business, and community called "Moscato and Tea." Her debut release of *Antonio and Sabrina Struck in Love* has opened a new avenue of writing that she loves. Nominated for 2021 Author of the Year, Best Black Romance "Mutual Agreement," and Best Interracial Romance for "She's All In Need". In 2022 nominated Author Queen of the Year, Best Black Romance "Nasir" Best Interracial Romance "Torn" and Best Romantic Comedy "Something Gained" by Black Girls Who Write.

If you want to know when the next book will come out, please visit my website at http://www.chiquitaden nie.com, where you can sign up to receive an email for my next release.

What's Next?

Want to know what happens next?

Follow me on social media to catch the next release.

Reviews are the lifeblood of the publishing world. They're read, appreciated, and needed. Please consider taking the time to leave a few words on Goodreads, or bookbub.

Sign up for updates and sneak peaks at the site below.

https://www.bookbub.com/chiquitadennie

https://www.chiquitadennie.com

https://www.goodreads.com/author/chiquitadennie

https://Facebook.com/chiquitassteamyreadinggroup

x.com/authorchiquitad

https://www.instagram.com/authorchiquitadennie

https://www.Facebook.com/authorchiquitadennie

https://www.304publishing.tumblr.com

Acknowledgments

A huge thank you to my team that helps me behind the scenes, from my editors, test readers, graphic designers, and the list goes on. Truly appreciate each of you for keeping me on my toes.

304 Publishing Company

We showcase authors writing Romance, Women's Fiction, Thriller, and Erotic.Along with Mystery, Suspense, Poetry, Beauty, and Style Books. Thank you for taking the time out to visit. Join our mailing list to stay updated with new releases and blog posts.

www.ingramcontent.com/pod-product-compliance
Lightning Source LLC
Chambersburg PA
CBHW011137190726
48289CB00012B/3066